Wish You Were Here

JOHN GIFFORD

ISBN: 978-0-9965405-5-1

Printed in the United States of America

Front Cover Photo: John Gifford
Author Photo: Wendy Mutz

Stories in this volume originally appeared, some in slightly different form and with different titles, in the following publications: *The Saturday Evening Post, Battle Runes: Writings on War* (Editions Bibliotekos), *Sleet Magazine, Cold Mountain Review, Carbon Culture Review, Storm Cellar, Harpur Palate, North Dakota Quarterly Mobile, The Los Angeles Review, Steam Ticket, Cloudbank, The Avalon Literary Review, Literary Juice, Portland Review, december, The Bluestone Review, Written River, The Ocean State Review, The MacGuffin, r.kv.r.y. quarterly, Kindred, The Sand Canyon Review, Ottawa Arts Review, Switchback,* and *Coastlines,* University of Southern Mississippi Gulf Coast.

Big Table Publishing Company
Boston, MA
www.bigtablepublishing.com

Acknowledgments

In addition to the editors of the literary magazines who have published my work, I'd like to express my gratitude to Gladys Lewis, who challenged me to write my first short-short story in her Ernest Hemingway seminar at the University of Central Oklahoma; to David Macey, whose opinions and careful judgment helped validate my work; and to my colleagues in UCO's MFA program, especially Roy Giles, Paula Sophia, and Noah Milligan, whose feedback helped tremendously in my development as a writer, and to RJ Woods, who introduced me to the format of short-short fiction and the power these miniature stories can have. Also, I wish to thank my editor, Robin Stratton, for believing in this project, and Jonathan Starke for his wise counsel and input on some of these pieces. I'm grateful, as well, to the Reverend Al Poteat for his friendship and guidance. Most of all, I'd like to express my heartfelt appreciation to my wife, Ellen, and my son, Jackson, for their steadfast love, support, and encouragement over the years. I love you.

Table of Contents

I

II

III

This book is for Ellen
With love

I

Provisions

At a sun-beaten, tin-roof shack along a busy dirt lane just outside Nairobi, a barefoot man in a crisp white shirt and dark shorts stands over a tub of iced fish, fanning flies. In his hand is a fly whisk made of goat hair and leather, which once belonged to his grandfather in the days before Mau Mau. The year "1963" has been carved into its handle–Kenya's year of independence, and also the birth year of his father who died at the age of twenty-five in a Nairobi rice riot.

The man's name is Jomo and leaning against the wall behind him is a large bag of Pishori rice–a succulent, long-grain variety, the pride of Kenya–which is open, the top neatly folded back and containing a metal can as a scoop. A piece of cardboard tacked to the wall above it reads:

~~160 Kenyan shillings per kilogram~~
~~140 shillings/kilogram~~
~~110 shillings~~
90 KSh

A man enters the shack. "Have you any sardines?" he asks in a British accent.

"I can get them," Jomo says, holding the fly whisk. He swats at the flies congregating around the fish and the movement calls to mind the image of his father swatting him with this same fly whisk for some infraction or another many years earlier. Often, this recollection leaves him feeling lonely and vulnerable. Today, however, he feels like smiling, yet he suppresses the urge. "It may take a few days," he says. "I can make you a good bargain on this seafood. That is Nile perch there. Just in from Tanzania."

"I'm headed out to the bush. No way to keep it," the Englishman says. "Oranges, perhaps?"

"Not this time of year," Jomo says. Then, pointing the fly whisk: "There is a mango available. And of course we have rice. Lots of rice."

"No sardines, no oranges. I reckon I came to the wrong place."

Jomo holds up his hand. "Please," he says, stepping to the corner of the shack and removing a bottle of Tusker beer from a box. He retrieves a bottle opener, pries off the lid and hands the warm beer to the Englishman. "Enjoy," he says.

"Many thanks," the Englishman says, lifting the bottle to his lips.

A boy enters the shack. Seeing him, Jomo smiles, hands him the fly whisk and points to the table, where the boy takes up a position and begins swatting at the flies buzzing around the fish.

"Is he your son?" the man says.

"This is my son, Kagunda. He is seven," Jomo says, his eyes lingering on the boy, then drifting to the table. There is a mud patch on the floor beneath the tub of fish, formed by the melting ice and growing in size, drop by drop, with the rising temperature. He turns to the Englishman, who is lighting a pipe. "Today I can make you

12

a great bargain on the fish. With some salt and ice, I am sure it would keep."

"I'm afraid of the heat, mate," the Englishman says, puffing on his pipe. "Isn't it risky to buy fish in this heat?"

"Every day is a risk when you operate your own business," Jomo says.

The man shakes his head, cradles the pipe in his fingers. "Have you always run this market?"

"Before this I worked at a candle factory for thirteen years," Jomo says. "I oversaw production. But I never once made a decision on my own. Nothing was done without approval from the front office."

"That's how it is working for the man, using your back and brains to make him rich."

Jomo considers this remark for a moment, remembering his grandfather and the stories he told of the British occupation in the days before Kenya's independence. "I do not enjoy taking risks," he says, "but at least the decision to do so is mine. I treasure that."

Kagunda moves away from the table and meanders around the shack, stopping in front of the shelf, where he swats at the flies buzzing around the mango.

The Englishman swirls the beer around in the bottle. "I appreciate the beer, mate," he says. "And no worries about the sardines. There's another market just down the road."

"If everyone thought like that, I would be out of business," Jomo says, grinning.

"I suppose so," the Englishman says.

13

"It is not easy running a market these days," Jomo says, motioning for Kagunda to return to his post at the table. "My competitors, the larger markets, the foreign shops, they have more resources. It is easy for them to stock everything. But me? I promise only what I can deliver."

"There's a word for that," the Englishman says. "Honesty?"

Jomo smiles. "I call it survival," he says.

The Englishman points with his pipe. "How is this Pishori rice?"

"It is a long-grain rice with excellent flavor. Very sweet. Locally grown," Jomo says. He lifts the bag and hefts it across the shack to the table where the lighting is better. Dropping it beside the fish, he grabs a handful of the grains and lets them sift through his hand, tiny pieces of home. "A beautiful rice of substance," he says. "Non-perishable."

"Real African rice?"

"This is one thing no one seems to be able to take from Kenya."

Movement catches Jomo's eye and instinctively, reflexively, he strikes as if holding the fly whisk. Realizing his folly, he drops his arm, his hand feeling the familiar leather handle, worn smooth from age and use, and he watches, aggravated, as the fly buzzes away, turns and comes again. He looks at Kagunda, pointing, and his son, fly whisk in hand, swats at the flies, once, twice, three times.

Beneath the table, the mud patch is growing.

"Today I could make you a tremendous deal on this fish," Jomo says to the Englishman. "It is fresh."

"I just don't have a need for it, mate. I appreciate your offer, and the beer. You've been very kind."

"Or the rice. It is a bargain at this price."

The Englishman tightens his lips, slowly shakes his head. "Maybe next time, mate," he says. "Just need a bloody tin of sardines."

Jomo crosses his arms, places a hand over his mouth, still feeling the smooth leather in his hand, the sharp *whisk-whisk* on his back side.

He motions to Kagunda and steps outside the shack, into the sun. When Kagunda comes out, Jomo takes the fly whisk and runs his fingers over the goat hair, straightening it, absorbing its texture, its history. Now speaking in Swahili, he gives the fly whisk back to his son, his hand lingering on the leather handle a moment before relinquishing it to the boy. He then points down the lane and the boy sprints away, and Jomo, remembering his father sending him on errands of his own, looks after the boy until he disappears into the dusty haze, into the throng of people moving up and down the road.

The Englishman steps out of the shack. "Thanks again, mate," he says.

Jomo holds up his hand. "Please," he says.

After the Land Run

Stars twinkle like fragments of gold glittering in a miner's pan as I lay here listening to the fire fizzle, embers popping and sizzling like bacon in a skillet. Out there in the dark, our claim flag flutters in the warm, spring breeze, snapping to attention with the gusts. I confess I took the flag from your curtains, cut it ragged and free, just like this new territory they carved out of these plains. Curtains that wait on a window to fill, a supper to shade, anyhow. And we had to stake our claim. Listen to the coyotes across the river, yipping and howling like school chums headed to town with two dollars in their pockets. I'm sorry about your curtains, but this land is ours now. And while you and the kids sleep, I'm counting the cost of coal oil, lumber, a mule to turn this prairie into pasture, this hillock into a home.

Chance of Rain

For thirty-nine days the temperature in the desert had peaked at one hundred and fifteen degrees. But on the fortieth day, clouds moved in and choked out the sunlight. The temperature struggled to reach ninety. That evening, the weatherman broadcasting on the Armed Forces Radio Network called for a fifty-percent chance of rain.

Through the door of the tent, Richard Juergens noticed lightning flashes in the sky. He and his machine gunner, Corporal Ramsey, were paired up against two other soldiers from the First Battalion in a game of spades. The men were sitting on cots inside the tent. Richard Juergens was about to throw down a card when the early-warning siren erupted. Lightning flashed in the sky. The lights in the tent blinked and then went out.

"Dude!" Ramsey said. "I had a good hand."

"Dude, get your gas mask on," Richard Juergens said. He removed his mask from the canvas pouch around his waist and pulled the straps over his head. With the rubber mask covering his face, he inhaled. Air rushed in through the filters. He felt the mask seal against his jawbone. "Got it on?"

Ramsey didn't answer. He had run to the door, where he stood looking out into the night.

"Ramsey, quit screwing around and get your mask on."

"I don't have it."

"You better have it," Richard Juergens said. "You

know you're not supposed to go anywhere without it."

"I think I left it at the chow hall," Ramsey said. "I sat it on the bench beside me and forgot to take it when we left."

"Don't you take anything seriously?" He shouted to project his voice beyond the rubber barrier insulating his face. "Always have your gas mask with you. That was an order from the colonel. And me."

Richard Juergens walked to the door where Ramsey was still looking up into the sky. Soldiers were running back and forth in the corridor between the tents. The siren continued wailing. It reminded him of the tornado sirens that sounded each spring in Texas and the noise gave him goose bumps on his neck and arms.

"Supply ships in port today," someone said. "That's why they're gunning for us."

Richard Juergens turned and walked back through the tent. He checked to make sure every man had his gas mask on. Then he looked at Ramsey and said, "Come on. We're going to get your mask."

But before they were out the door, two explosions sounded, shaking the wooden frame of the tent. The noise reverberated through Richard Juergens' head, down his spine, rattling the fillings in his teeth.

"Patriots are up," someone else said. "That SCUD's headed our way."

"Everybody get down behind the sandbags and keep your heads down," Richard Juergens said. He looked toward the door. In the illumination from a lightning flash, he saw Ramsey kneeling beside one of the cots. Ramsey's head was bowed and his hands were clasped together near his chin.

Just then a voice came over the loudspeaker outside, shouting, *Gas, gas, gas!*

Richard Juergens walked over to Ramsey and put a hand on his shoulder. He could feel the corporal shaking.

"I never got my anthrax shot!" he said.

"You're kidding me!"

"I wish."

"You lied to me. You told me you got it. What's wrong with you?" Richard Juergens felt the acid boiling in his stomach. He could hear soldiers running outside the tent, their boots striking the ground and kicking at the sandbags as they scrambled over the barricade. *Gas, gas, gas!* the voice continued over the loudspeaker. "Why didn't you get your shot? You knew this could happen."

"I was afraid of the side effects," he said. In the lightning flashes, Richard Juergens could see the sweat glistening on Ramsey's face. He could see the whites of his eyes glowing. His Adam's apple jiggled as he talked. "The corpsman said it's only been tested on cows. I ain't a damn cow! What if I get cancer or something?"

"What if you don't live long enough to get cancer?" Richard Juergens said. "We're going to get your mask."

"I don't think we should risk it."

"You willing to bet the missile won't fall on us? You willing to bet it's not dirty?"

Ramsey, sitting on the edge of the cot, buried his face

in his hands. The lightning flashed and Richard Juergens saw the cards scattered on the plywood crate they had used as a table. Playing spades had been Ramsey's idea. Robert Juergens wasn't a gambler; he didn't even know how to play the game until Ramsey taught him. He'd told him they could win some money.

"I don't like to lose money," Richard Juergens had said.

"We have a good chance of winning," Ramsey had told him. "I feel good about it."

Now, listening to the sounds of the rain beginning to pelt the heavy canvas tent, peppering the sandbags on the bunker walls just outside the door, falling loudly, forcefully, inevitably, Richard Juergens closed his eyes and whispered a prayer behind the protection of the rubber mask that sealed his face from an uncertain future.

Ramsey stood up from the cot and said, "I hate this. I hate not being able to do anything. I don't even want to think about what's going to happen if those Patriots miss and that SCUD hits us."

Richard Juergens broke the seal on his gas mask, pulled it from his head and felt the air suddenly cool and invigorating on his face. With the mask off, his vision was clear and sharp. "You better not think about it then," he said. "Here. Put it on and let's get down by those sandbags."

Two Turtledoves

On my last evening in Tripoli, the air humid and thick, I stuffed my pocket with a little cash and headed for the bustling souk to find something to eat. There, in a cobblestone-lined alleyway glowing with hot braziers and spinning Shawarma spits, the scent of grilled meat in the air, and surrounded by rawboned vendors offering olives, dates, leather shoes, spices, gold jewelry, wool rugs, tin ornaments, baked goods, and intricately designed tiles, wall coverings, dishes, I came upon a man selling birds. His flimsy cage flitted with the movement of orioles, warblers, and a single turtledove, its cinnamon wings delicate and flaky. It tilted its head and looked at me through a red-ringed eye, a neon door to its heart. I snuffed out my cigarette, shaking my head, saddened by the sight of hopeless captivity amid all this life.

Seeing my reaction, the man running the stall stood. "You Americans love your wars but cry over animals," he said. "Where is your sympathy when the bombs are falling?"

The turtledove was cooing now. I watched it watch me from behind the red peephole.

Before I could respond to the man, before I could tell him that not all Americans believe in dropping bombs, that our sympathy is always with the victims, he stepped up and gestured toward his captives. "These birds," he said, placing a meaty hand on the cage, scattering the birds. "They are what we eat when the bombs are falling on our cities and fields." Then, grinning: "And when they are not!"

I might have argued with the man. I might have protested. I might have thrown a fit and called him cruel or savage, cracked the cage and freed the birds myself. But that wouldn't have stopped this deplorable practice.

My hand moved to the cigarettes in my shirt pocket, then fell away.

The man had retreated to the back of the stall and he reemerged now with something in his hands. His attention on the birds, a look of expectation on his face, he made a tossing motion with one arm, then the other. Dark clouds formed above the cage and instantly dissipated as seed rained down through the wire. "Eat! Eat while you can!" he said, laughing as the grain shower caused the traumatized birds to explode into flight, into a discordant flock of frenetic feathers bouncing off the wire walls, like hot popcorn in a bag.

Then the real rain began, striking the ground in a slow staccato drumbeat before organizing into a steady assault. As vendors rushed to cover their wares, the bird man melted into the depths of his stall, where he lit a cigarette.

Exposed, the birds huddled together in the cage, trying to preserve body heat.

I slapped all my cash down on the table, then removed the pack of cigarettes from my shirt pocket and sweetened the deal. I told myself I was finished as I reached for the cage door.

This is Why We're Going

They're writing songs about it. They're making movies about it. Not because someone says they have to. It's because they want to. You see that pickup truck across the river? The hombre who owns it decided that's what he wanted. So he walked into the pickup truck store, pointed with his finger and said, Give me that one, even though he could have bought this one or that other one, see. And get this: the man–or the woman. Could have been a woman–who built it said, I want a job making pickup trucks. There's nobody telling him he has to build trucks. He does it because he wants to. If he wanted to, he could be running a market somewhere, or fixing people's teeth, or laying the bricks on these new homes they're building up in Texas. They tell me there's lots of work in Texas. You can work every day if you want. Me, I want Sundays off. But every other day I'm going to stay hooked up. That's how you do it, see. These men you hear about, the ones with their own pickup trucks, with new boots and pretty wives? They've already figured this out, see. That's why we're going. When I'm old and my teeth fall out, I want to know that what they put in there is better than what I started with.

Money Note

At 3:15 they call my son, Mark, into the studio for his audition. He's spent the last year preparing for this moment, a year of actor's training and private voice lessons. It's expensive, but the cost doesn't matter. It's all worth it as long as Mark is having fun.

He's been working with Lenny Thomas, the Broadway star. You'd be surprised what kind of fees he gets. But that's not important. I just want Mark to enjoy himself. That's all that matters.

Today the theater company is auditioning for *Aladdin* and, I know I'm his mother, but I think Mark would be perfect as the prince. Believe me: I've made sure the director knows he's working with Lenny Thomas.

I'd love to see Mark succeed in theater. It never worked out for me. But Mark's good enough. I want him to go all the way to Broad—really, this is *his* thing. He can do what he wants with it.

Look at me. I'm so keyed up. I'd love a cigarette right now, but I've stopped.

I hand Mark his headshot and résumé, and pat his hand. "Sweetie, whatever happens is fine," I say, trying to appear calm and collected so he'll relax. If he's relaxed, he'll nail the audition. I know he will. "Just have fun with it."

He turns and walks into the studio without saying anything. All the other kids are watching. He's a nervous wreck. But he'll nail it. We've been practicing at home.

"What part does Mark want?" says Verna, one of the other mothers. I like Verna, but you try talking to her about *anything*—movies, food, the weather—and she'll steer the conversation back to theater. That's all she wants to talk about.

"Whatever he gets," I say with a wave of my hand. Glancing around the waiting room, I look at each of the eight other eleven-year-old boys competing for a part in the show. I'm sure they all want to be the prince, but none of them seem to fit the part, if you ask me. There are a lot more girls but I don't worry about them. "He's just happy to be in the show. What about Lucas?"

"Oh, he's still learning the fundamentals. He probably won't even get in."

"Mark probably won't either," I tell her. "I wish he'd go out for basketball, tall as he is."

"Looks like it could get bad this afternoon," Verna says, pointing to the television on the wall. The weatherman has his jacket off and his sleeves rolled up. "They're calling for severe storms."

"Those weathermen sure get worked up, don't they?" I say as I stand from my seat. "I'm going to see if he can even carry a note."

"Oh, your son can sing," Verna says. "We heard him at the last audition. I wish Lucas could sing like him."

"You're sweet to say that."

The piano is already playing in the studio. I place my ear against the door, following Mark as he sings, listening,

25

waiting for the money note he's been working on. There, there it is! Yes, he nailed it!

How could they not give him Aladdin?

I float back to my seat.

"He sounded great," Verna says. "I wish Lucas could sing like that."

"Aren't you sweet."

Verna shifts in her seat and leans forward. "If you don't mind me asking, what did you have to pay for his voice lessons?"

"Oh, I don't even remember," I say. "I don't think it was very much."

The studio door opens and a girl comes out. "Lucas. You ready?"

"Remember what we worked on," Verna says, handing her son his headshot and résumé.

"Good luck, Lucas," I say.

Mark takes a seat beside me on the bench.

"You sounded great!" Verna says. Then she stands. "Guess I'll see if mine can remember his lyrics." She walks to the studio and places her ear to the door as the piano accompaniment begins.

"Did you smile like we talked about?" I say.

"I think so," Mark says.

"Did you relax your shoulders like Lenny taught you?" I keep asking him questions because I have to know. He sounded strong to me, but I wasn't in the room with him.

Before I know it, Verna is coming back.

"He sounded good," I say. "He'd be great as the prince."

"Oh, thank you," she says. Then, pointing again to the television: "Better put your car in the garage tonight. Looks like we could get some hail."

"These weathermen," I say, shaking my head. "You can't believe half of what they say."

Lucas appears and takes a seat beside Verna.

"Nice going in there," I say. "Now the waiting begins, huh?"

"Waiting's the worst," he says.

"You're right about that," I say. Then, turning to Mark: "I need to call the office. Be right back."

Outside, I climb into the car, crack the window and light a cigarette–my first in two days. I inhale deeply, holding it, savoring the kick, as I pull out my phone and call my husband, Brad.

"He nailed it. Sixteen hundred dollars of lessons are paying off," I say. "I know he's going to get the prince. I just know it."

"You watching the weather?" he says. "There's a storm going up just south of you. Maybe you should head home."

"They know he's been working with Lenny Thomas," I say, the cigarette smoldering in my fingers. "I don't know how they couldn't give him the prince."

7:51 a.m.

It begins not as a flash, but as a faint, warm glow in the east. Just then a narrow, golden-yellow brushstroke appears on the sleepy gray canvas of ground, the first sign of the artist at work and the impending scene now taking shape. Already it is warm and true and distinct, this single shaft of soft illumination, a moment of hope soon to be realized, a deft promise that glows and grows, glows and grows, growing, warming away the thin blanket of hoarfrost, melting the solid, frosty sheen into a sparkling dew, silent and still, and resplendent in its fleeting spotlight. And now the long stillness begins to recede with the first flicker of movement in the trees, the first ebullient whistles of good-morning cheer, as the chilly musicians descend from their lofts and take their places on lower branches, larger branches, beneath the dormant brambles and briars, bathed now in the warm, slowly expanding spotlight as the picture comes to life, and time, like the scene taking shape with every new brushstroke, each brighter and bolder than the last, never stops advancing.

This is What it Means to Believe

It was the last Sunday of the revival at the Tabernacle and Pastor Bill, who was dressed in a white suit, his wild mane of silver hair pomaded and tamed, had just led the congregation in a particularly spirited rendition of the old gospel song, "I Shall Not Be Moved," when, to my surprise, he stepped up to the pulpit, reached into the wooden box and pulled out a big timber rattler, which he held up in the air. The crowd in the tent that day let out a collective gasp as Pastor Bill, whose cheeks and forehead glistened with perspiration, said The Lord was speaking to him, was telling him to touch the serpent, was telling him to take it out of the box and hold it up as a sign of his faith. Those rattles must have been three inches long and I could feel their vibrating deep down in my bones, even though I stood several rows back from the rostrum, between my wispy cousin, Sonya, who was wavering like she was going to faint, and my Aunt Louise, who had lured me to the revival with the promise of her sweet lemonade, and my Uncle Ike's barbecue, afterward. Pastor Bill was standing there with his eyes closed, holding the snake above his head, when someone shouted "Praise the Lord!" and the rattling quickened. Then, with the crowd of men, women, and children watching, the tension as thick as the timber rattler's scaly body, sweat beads slipping down Pastor Bill's cheeks like water trickling from spring seeps, the rattling intensified yet again until it seemed the entire tent was vibrating. Aunt Louise gasped. Cousin Sonya latched onto my arm. Then there was a sharp hissing sound as the snake lunged and struck, biting Pastor Bill's left hand. It happened in a flash. By the time I realized what was going on, the snake was back in the box and the deacons were converging on Pastor Bill, whose face was as white as his suit as he clutched his bitten hand and backed away from the pulpit. A moment later he was seated on the edge of the rostrum, his right hand clamped to his left wrist as twin beads of blood oozed and dripped onto his white suit just above the knee. The agitated crowd massed around the pastor like a human blood clot. "Ambulance is on the way," someone said. Then, Pastor Bill, his face pale and sweaty, but calm, said, "There's no need. The Lord wanted me to handle that snake and he'll see me through." Sister Myrna, his wife, leaned over and gave him a hug, tears streaming down her cheek. Then she looked at him and said, "Sweetheart, that was a big snake." Pastor Bill, his hair still perfect, blood still dripping onto his white suit, and now seemingly winded, shook his head. "It's okay, Baby Doll. I got a big faith."

Breathe

My brother's asthma attacks would come in the night, while I was sleeping, and I'd awaken to my mother helping Alex out of bed and into his clothes as he coughed and rasped and wheezed, his lungs straining for air, starving for oxygen.

"Where's your inhaler?" she would whisper, trying to avoid waking everyone else. "Use your inhaler."

Alex responded in between breaths, his voice hoarse. "I did."

One night I sat up in bed to let my mother know I was awake. I was mildly concerned for Alex, though he was sick so much of the time that I had grown used to seeing him like this. I had grown complacent at his condition and that's because I couldn't appreciate what it felt like to not be able to breathe.

"Use it again," she said. Then, to me: "I'm taking your brother to the hospital. You go back to sleep."

"I can't sleep," I said.

Scoof, scoof, came the sounds of Alex's inhaler. He took a deep breath, his lungs rattling, straining from the effort. And then silence as he held his breath for five seconds, ten, and not much more. He exhaled and began gasping for air as if he'd just jogged a couple miles, even though, with his asthma, this was something he couldn't do.

"If you're coming with us, hurry up," my mother said.

I cared nothing for hospitals, but I was awake, and curious. So I got out of bed and dressed, then followed my brother through the house, careful to not wake my father and three sisters. We walked out to the car. Alex and I got into the back seat and my mother pulled out of the driveway and zipped through the neighborhood, rolling the stop signs and surging through intersections with barely a sideways glance. Porch lights glowed from the houses we passed, illuminating empty yards, the slumbering silhouettes of parked cars and trucks. Everything was quiet and still. Except for Alex's labored breathing. Except for the car's racing engine.

I could hear the carburetor sucking air when my mother pressed the gas, and it seemed to me that all that good air was being wasted on a car.

Alex didn't say anything. He seemed consumed with the task of breathing, which to me was baffling. Sitting beside him in the back seat, watching Alex's slumping silhouette rocking slowly back and forth, as if this gentle motion might help him take in more oxygen, I wondered how the function of breathing could be so easy and effortless for me, and yet so laborious for him. It wasn't fair. Alex hadn't done anything wrong and yet he spent so much of his life struggling to breathe, struggling to do something I took for granted.

He coughed and this interrupted his respiratory rhythm, which intensified the struggle and which heralded a convulsing, coughing fit that seemed to prolong the drive to the hospital, that seemed to arrest our efforts to get there.

I closed my eyes and prayed. I prayed for Alex to be

able to breathe. I prayed that I could help him.

"Roll your window down, Honey," my mother said from the driver's seat. Then, to me: "Help your brother roll his window down. He needs air."

The open window amplified the sounds of the racing engine, the rushing air. I could feel the car accelerate, hear the whoosh of the exhaust as we barreled through the empty streets, barely slowing for the flashing red lights at intersections. At one point the street lights around us seemed to intensify, pulsate, and finally blur into one continuous stream of bright yellow light illuminating the car seats, my brother's jeans, his shoes, and his pale, skinny hand pushing against his knee to support the weight of his slumping body. I wondered for a moment if I was dreaming. Then I heard a police siren.

"No!" my mother said. "I don't have time for this!"

"Just take a deep breath, Mom," I said, repeating the advice she often gave me.

Alex looked at me through his thick glasses. "Wish I could," he said between breaths.

I almost burst out laughing even though I was simultaneously frustrated and saddened for Alex. For a ten-year-old kid, he could be quite witty, and humorous, even in the most somber of circumstances. Once, after his mini-bike was stolen out of the garage, a police officer had stopped by the house to take a report. Alex told the officer that he had seen a couple of kids eyeing the miniature motorcycle earlier that day, and that whomever had taken it was in for a surprise. "They think they got a mini-bike," he said. "But what they really got was a money pit. Gas is over a dollar a gallon these days."

Maybe it was his way of saying he was going to be all right, or letting us know asthma might have his lungs, but not his spirit. Regardless, Alex was struggling to breathe and it wasn't the time for levity. So I contained my laughter by turning and looking through the back window at the flashing red-and-blue lights moving in behind us.

My mother cranked the window down. "My son can't breathe!" she shouted. "He's having an asthma attack. We're headed to the hospital."

The officer shined a light into the back seat. Alex sat hunched over, his bony shoulders visible beneath his T-shirt, his back rising and falling, his breathing shallow and raspy.

"Ma'am, I'll give you an escort," the officer said. "Follow me."

We raced through the empty streets even faster than before, the officer's flashing lights leading the way, leading us left and right and onward to the hospital, to steroids and breathing treatments for my brother, and a steady respiratory rate, a breath of air for which he needn't struggle, or even think about. Until the next asthma attack.

Years later, as an adult, Alex would outgrow his asthma. He grew so big that sometimes it was hard to believe he had ever struggled to breathe, healthy as he was.

He even wanted to follow me into the Marines. In his letters, he told me he planned on joining in the fall, after he finished high school. But I talked him out of it, remembering his skinny profile slumped over in the back seat of my mother's car, rocking back and forth, his breathing raspy and rough as he fought for air. I told him about the gas chamber, about them closing the door and locking us in there, and the drill instructors yelling at us to remove our gas masks—those awkward rubber masks they had issued us, which no one cared for, cumbersome and ugly as they were—and lift our arms high above our heads, and trying to hold my breath, feeling the CS gas burning my face and neck, my eyes, burning hot, rough and scratchy, and stinging, like someone had sprayed me with hairspray and then lit a match, and finally expelling the air from my lungs and gasping for more, but feeling, tasting, CS gas as my eyes blurred, as my nose drained, and the drill instructors with gas masks over their faces yelling at us to keep our hands up and telling us not to run for the door but to stand fast and breathe, breathe, suck in the gas, the burning gas, and coughing, choking, fighting for air, waiting, wondering if I would pass out, wondering if I would die, and then finally, *finally*, hearing the order to don and clear our gas masks and feeling the strap on my head as I pulled that wonderful device over my face.

I inhaled sharply and felt the thick rubber suck up against my cheeks and jawbone, creating a seal against the gas. My eyes were still watery, my nose snotty, and my neck and hands burned, as before. But now I could breathe. I could breathe!

Then there was daylight, glorious daylight, as they opened the door. We marched out into the cool air and removed our masks. Several of the recruits, as if intoxicated by the fresh air, and staggering around with hands on their hips, flung their masks to the ground. But I clung to mine. I took one deep breath and then another, and as I reveled in the clean air, in the oxygen, in life, my mind went back to childhood, to my brother and his asthma attacks, to watching Alex struggle to breathe that night as we raced through the streets under police escort on the way to the hospital.

Back at the barracks that evening, while the other recruits were cleaning weapons or writing letters, I rinsed and cleaned my gas mask, careful to keep the filters dry. Then, using a soft T-shirt, I polished the eyepieces until they were clear and bright. Afterwards, I carefully folded the mask and returned it to its case. Sitting on the edge of my bunk, I held it a moment, studying it, feeling the heft of its reassurance inside the smooth canvas case.

Rather than hanging it on the corner post of my bunk with my other web gear, I walked over to my footlocker, lifted the lid, and placed it in the top tray, beside my Bible and letters from home.

Too Nice to Drop

At first, I had trouble buttoning my shirts. I'd spend minutes on a single button, trying to push that pearly disc through the slit, only to end up frustrated, in tears, or worked up into such a fit that I was ready to throw my guitar out the window. It's a six-string Martin with rosewood neck and mother-of-pearl inlays. Everyone loves it. My wife, Claire, gave it to me when I finished my master's degree, just before the doctors diagnosed me with MS. I always wanted a Martin, but I can't enjoy it. It's like I'm wearing gloves. My fingers touch the strings, but I can't feel them. I play on instinct. Whenever I pick up my instrument my fingers just go to their places, like actors on a stage.

The university doesn't know. Back when they hired me, I could feel the strings. I could feel the chords I see in my mind. Now my fingers make the chords, but I can't feel them.

I don't know how much longer I can keep this secret. The drugs aren't helping. They cause me to laugh uncontrollably, or make me sleepy. My doctor says the stuff I'm on now could distort my perception of reality. At least I don't have to cancel class every time I hear a good joke. Claire says I look tired. She says I look tired and worried. I guess I am. At night, I dream she's pushing me around in a wheelchair. I know that's what's coming. Already, I've had to give up driving. After my second fender-bender, Claire said it was time to hand over the keys, even though my insurance agent refused to terminate my policy. He said I've been one of his best customers over the years. Going around without a car has been a blessing, though, because it's given me more time to focus on my students. Now all I have to do is teach, and try not to fall. That's the hard part. I used to never fall. Now I stumble every day–the wrong chord here, a missed step there. I would have given up by now if not for my students and colleagues. They're big-hearted people and I hate deceiving them like this. A few of them even follow me around between classes, probably hoping to pick up a tip here and there to help them play better. When I start to fall, they run up and catch me. "We don't want anything bad to happen," they say, their eyes strumming my guitar. "We're just trying to help." But I know what they're thinking, and I don't blame them. It's a Martin, after all.

Even Lifetime Warranties Have Expiration Dates

Not long into your journey, a journey you haven't prepared for, one that, because you have no specific destination in mind has caused you to question your very origin–the where, the how, the why, the when–you realize you're lost, that you have no idea what you're doing or why you're doing it. You stop for directions in a tired, somber town that is rendered even more austere by the eye-squinting brilliance of a brand new day. A faded sign says the town was built during the gold rush at the turn of the century, and now, less than a hundred years later, it's teetering on the edge of this life, and eternity.

Just across the pockmarked highway is a lush, verdant field humming with life. There are constellations of wildflowers, bouquets of singing birds, and a clear-running stream full of rainbow trout. Purple mountains loom in the distance, their snow-capped peaks sparkling white in the sun and looking clean and new. They remind you of something.

Now a man wearing a hardhat and carrying a hammer appears before you. Very calmly, he explains the way home. It's not easy, he warns. You'll be tempted to take the wrong turn here, the wrong road there. Do as I say, however, and you'll get home.

But you're not paying attention. You're listening instead to another man who has crept up behind you. He is complimenting you on your shoes, your watch, your shiny new car. It's as perfect as the sky, he says.

Not for long, says the man in the hardhat.

Promotion Day

Don't view it as a sacrifice. It's a responsibility. It's tradition. So stop thinking about the pain. Stop wondering how many of the guys were Golden Gloves boxers. Stop thinking about yourself and accept your obligation. Nobody made you join. You asked for the chance to become a Marine. You became a Marine. You are a Marine. Three years in The Suck and you've finally made corporal. So smile. Relax. Listen to the captain as he reads your promotion warrant. And get ready for fourteen of your buddies to pin your stripes on you. Remember: you can't run. You can't flinch. You can't show any sign of weakness or the guys will have a field day on you. But why would you? You're a Marine. Marines maintain their bearing. You don't wince. You don't grimace. You walk through the gauntlet on promotion day. Head held high. Shoulders squared. You get your stripes pinned on. And when one of the other jarheads gets promoted, you form a gauntlet with the others. You make a fist. You watch. You wait. You aim for the arm. You aim for the shoulder. You haul back and knock fire out of him. Afterward, after he's made it through, you shake his hand. If he can't raise his arm to shake your hand, you tell him congratulations. You tell him you'll buy him a beer later. That'll get him to raise his arm. Put a beer in front of him. It works. It worked on you last time. Remember? It's a good thing promotions are so infrequent because, even though you're a Marine, you've got only two arms and it takes a while to recover. Maybe that's why, in the Marine Corps, they don't just hand them out. Maybe that's why, in the Marine Corps, you have to earn them. And then you pay for them. Which is what you're about to do as the captain steps in front of you now; as he hands your promotion warrant to the first sergeant; as he removes the metal chevrons from your collar and hands them away; as he takes the corporal chevrons from the first sergeant; as he slides the brass clasps off the sharp prongs; as he punches one, and then the other, into your collar; as he, with the brass clasps still in his hand and the sharp prongs exposed, brings his hands down onto the chevrons, driving the prongs through your utility blouse, through your cotton undershirt, through your young skin and into the hard muscle just beneath your collarbone. Remember: you're a Marine. Which is why you don't wince. Which is why you don't grimace. Which is why you remain at attention, eyes looking straight ahead but not focused on the captain, who is now slipping the safety clasps onto the sharp prongs on back of your new chevrons…until he offers his hand and says congratulations. Now you shake his hand. Now you contemplate his sharp, stinging grin grinning at you and your own grin—at least you think you feel a grin forming on your face. Now the captain is calling the platoon to attention. Now he's dismissing you. Now the other Marines, the corporals and above, fourteen of them, three of which were once Golden Gloves boxers, begin to grin their own grins and pound their fists against their open hands and laugh and taunt you as you approach the two lines, telling yourself that it's only fourteen punches, that it's only seven slugs on each arm, that the end of the gauntlet is only a few paces away, that after the first two or three hits your arms will go numb and you'll feel nothing, that it will probably be several years before you make sergeant and have to do this again, that Dad and Granddad did this same thing, that you yourself have done this same thing–twice–after your first two promotions, that you can do it again, that tonight you'll drink until you can't feel your arms anymore, that this–beer–is a pleasant thought, that this–beer–is such a pleasant thought that you focus on this–beer–and this–beer–alone: on beer, cold beer, cold salty beer swirling down your throat, making you warm and happy and numb, helping you forget that you're stepping now into the gauntlet, helping you forget that you're a Marine.

Worms

Before his wife left him, before the oil spill, when he was still working with the research institute out there on eighty-eight, he used to stop in here and buy these plastic swimming pools we sell for kids. Like that one over there. Only he and his wife didn't have any kids, see. They said he was growing something in his garage at home. I never believed he was a druggie. Had too good a job. Smart as hell, they said. Married the prettiest girl in town. Then that truck turned over and spilled that oil all over them woods out there by the lake. Next day he come in and cleaned us out of swimming pools. Then we heard his wife left him. Said he was raising worms. Had worms all over the garage. They were getting into the house, see. Someone said when she found one in her underwear drawer, why, she was done. Pretty little thing. We wondered why someone like him would want to fool with worms. Thought he might be getting into the bait business, but that didn't make sense, man smart as him. Pretty soon they said he'd left the research institute, was living out of his car. We thought he'd hit bedrock. Then we seen him on the five-o'clock news. They were covering the oil spill, you know, talking with locals, talking with the feds. They introduced him as a scientist who was using worms to clean up that mess. We about busted a gut laughing at that one. But he's the one laughing now. Swimming in all that money. His wife wanted him back, but he wouldn't take her. He's getting five-figure fees to go and talk about his worms. Talks to universities, scientific outfits. He's smart as hell. And to think we used to leave behind cans of Vienna sausages and sleeves of crackers in the campgrounds after our deer hunts, thinking he needed food. He knew what he was doing all along. He brought the tourists back to Leech Lake. Saved a lot of businesses here in town. I seen him on the cover of some magazine not long ago. The other day a reporter come in, just like you, asking if I know him. I said hell yes I know him. I knew that sonofagun when he was just a nobody, living in his car out in the woods. Reporter's eyes got this big. He pulled out that notebook, wanting to know if he could quote me. I said hell yes you can quote me for two hundred dollars, same as I charge everyone else. Same as you just paid me. And I'll tell you like I told him: for two hundred more, I'll take you out to the woods where he used to live in that car. I know right where it's at. Something else: I bet there's still some of them worms out there, squirming their way through life, living off what he gave them.

Refugees

Your body still haunts me. Sometimes, driving home of an afternoon, or during those long, bleak days of winter, when nightfall comes much too soon, and I'm at home, alone, sitting cross-legged on the floor, I think of you there in the passenger seat, only a few inches away, vacillating, giggling, your breath sticky-sweet as I slipped the shirt over your head and offered you mine, offered you gum, helping you slip the stick from the wrapper as you sat there looking out at the world as if for the first time—you, the one with the pep and spirit, most likely to succeed, my dream rider, now without a ticket to punch and strangely unsure of yourself. When the gum didn't work, we tried saltines, crumbling crackers like rice confetti marking the miles of a trail I could find blind, scratched record repeating with every revolution around town, resetting the needle, song skipping, resetting the needle, song skipping, music lost to the ages, and melodies, like the turntable and Long Play records, supplanted by something newer, replaced by something not necessarily better. Our time together was all too brief and before I knew it we were stepping up to your parents' house, your head on my shoulder, my shirt like a gown on your body as I stood you up, steadying your unsteady head, stuffing your vomit-splattered shirt into your hand, a hand I'd always wanted to hold, but never would. I pressed the doorbell and disappeared, leaving you alone, vulnerable to the loving arms of your parents' disapproval. You hadn't come to the party with me, but I couldn't let you drive home like that. You probably don't even remember, though I could never forget. Sometimes, I see you in line at the market. I see you in a beaming smile on TV. I see you in the impossibly tall hair I run my fingers through in my dreams. And sometimes I wonder: who's standing you up now?

Reception

They walked out of the store, the boy tapping and swiping the screen of his father's new phone. The father, holding the papers for the service plan he'd just signed, noticed a spot on the passenger side of his car. "A door ding, already?" he said, scowling, running his finger back and forth over the blemish. "It's pretty bad when you haven't even had your car three days and you get a door ding."

The boy, still tapping and swiping at the device in his hands, didn't seem to hear his father and never looked up.

Temple, Texas

Even years later, long after he'd crossed the Red River for the big job in Oklahoma, after he'd made VP and began to stuff his 401K like a trophy largemouth, after the kids had finished college and he could revel in the knowledge that retirement loomed on the horizon like daybreak, he was still collecting Fridays like postcards from home and he'd phone the office, tell them *Not today,* then straddle the big V-Twin and gallop hours south where he'd spend the day unzipping the central Texas farm roads, nodding as the ranchers passed him in their dusty trucks, noting the herds of polled Herefords and black Angus and Chianina, invigorated by the scent of alfalfa and buffalograss, counting the tumbleweeds tumbling past until his genetics could come out and breathe and he felt again the coyote satisfaction of wind-burned skin and the heat of the Texas sun branding his neck and, around suppertime, the nostalgic comfort of a Dairy Queen brazier burger on his tongue, mustache painted in peanut buster parfait and no one around to notice but the high-school girls behind the counter—"Yes, sir," they'd say—their smiles like a blanket of bluebonnets in April. Sometimes, he'd stay long enough to refill his lemonade and his wife would call and he'd forget and answer the phone, "Howdy."

Charmed

For a man like Frank, for someone his size—he was six foot, anyway; two hundred pounds or better—with all that strength and speed, and *intelligence*—had a college degree, Frank did, from Florida, where he'd played ball—and all the *Hey, look at me! Come over here!* of a magnet—everybody loved him: guys, girls, colonels; they all wanted to shake his hand and look at that ring—I couldn't understand why he didn't want to listen, why he didn't want to do like everybody else was doing and take that injection they said would save us if the enemy was to hit us with those chemicals everybody said they was stockpiling. I didn't doubt it, and I hadn't hesitated to get mine. It's not like I had a choice about it, anyhow. It's not like any of us had a choice. It wasn't our say. Wasn't none of us officers. Wasn't none of us free to make that kind of decision. They wouldn't let us forget that we was all government property, that our bodies didn't belong to us anymore. Frank wasn't no different than anybody else in that respect. He didn't have the authority to tell them no. Even with that college education of his, that ring, those shoulder muscles, big as bowling balls, even with all that Frank didn't have no more authority than any of the rest of us. But that didn't seem to faze him. That didn't make any difference to Frank. I didn't want to, but they made me talk to him. It's not like I knew any more about it than he did, but they made me go anyhow because I was his squad leader. I says, Frank, don't you want to feel safe if they shoot them chemicals at us? I says, don't you want keep off the colonel's radar? I says, don't you want to just do like the rest of us and whip our enemy so we can get back home? He says, Dobber, I don't want to cause no trouble, but I'm not taking it. He says, I don't know what they put in there and I don't want it in my body. I couldn't blame him. If I had a body like Frank's, a National Champions ring big as a brick on my finger, I wouldn't want to take any of that crap either. But I'm not Frank and, like they say, some of us get through life a little easier than others. Let me put it this way: if the colonel had called me into his office that day instead of Frank, you can bet your boots he wouldn't have stood from his desk when I walked in. He wouldn't have shook my hand. He wouldn't have asked me about my family, or if I liked the chow they was feeding us, or how it was playing for Urban Meyer.

The Wedding Singer

I recognized him soon as he stuck his head in the door, sold us that smile of his. He had this shine to him. Always did. That same bling as before. Gold rings on his fingers like the poker players wear. Diamond studs in his ears big as peanuts. The weird thing was, he recognized *me*. He said, "You're the dude gave us tickets to the Nuggets game that time!" The company had some extra tickets that year. He was in college then. That was twenty years ago, or more. I couldn't believe he remembered me. Anyway, he just slid into the conference room, a hundred and twenty of us sitting in there talking about the latest camouflage patterns, you know. Trying to decide what the next big thing was going to be. He said, "How you been?" Everybody knew who he was. He loved the attention. You could tell. Looked like he ought to be in Vegas, way he was dressed. Said he was looking for a wedding reception there in the building somewhere. Said he was supposed to be *singing*. I didn't know what to say. He was the best point guard in the NBA at one time. Now he's singing at weddings around the West. Anyway, he came over and I started to hand him the mike. He said, "Do me a favor." I said, "What?" "A favor," he said. He was whispering, trying to keep his voice down. Told me, "Say Ray, make it rain." I said, "Do what?" He said, "Say Ray, make it rain." I didn't know what he had in mind, but I did like he wanted. I said, "Ray, make it rain!" His face lit up like the Vegas strip. He smiled real big, tossed a wad of money that thick into the air. Everybody was clapping and carrying on. Crispy bills showering us like autumn leaves. Felt like I was on a game show. Ray was standing there beaming, just like in that parade that time after they won the championship. I still remember seeing that on TV. Then he waved, signed a few autographs, and walked out. Just like that. I looked down there at all those bills scattered around my feet. I didn't know if I should pick them up, try to give them back, or what. They were ones and fives mostly.

What Would Your Mother Say?

To find you a part of this crowd with the sun-seared skin, out here in the street with a car bumper bumping your chin? What would she say to see you staring down that big American engine, its humming economy fueled by your high-octane metabolism, cooled by the salt on your neck? What would she say to look out the door and see society honking and shouting, and you just sitting there, an inconvenient speed bump to negotiate, frozen like some D.C. frieze–familiar and yet so foreign? You wonder if the reporters are getting all this, if it's your face and disheveled hair your mother will see when she opens tomorrow's newspaper, whether she'll recognize you in that split second before she crumples the paper and cleans the nation's glass. Will she understand? Or will she see it as just another of your foolish stunts? What would she say now, to see you thrashing and resisting, shouting to the cameras as they drag you across the grass? You know exactly what she'd say. The only thing she told you to do was to keep your mouth shut.

III

Rewired

We used to see him all the time: dressed for the cold on a hot summer day, bag in his hands as he made his way along the street, a crackling charge circulating through the city on a closed-circuit tour of his own hometown. He always seemed oblivious to the jeers and catcalls from across the street, the group of boys regarding him in a concerted stare, wide-eyed and jumpy, as he marched along, headed who knew where, garbled words spewing from his lips like exhaust from an engine with misfiring ignition.

But what grounded him to our minds was not the fierce expression he wore on his face, or the brown paper bag he carried, or the amped-up way he marched around town, but rather his hands, which were always balled into fists, as if ready to swing and fight on the very next step.

Yet, for all the attention his hands generated from the fascinated public, a public that always stopped whatever it was doing to watch him, but which he himself never appeared to notice, no one I knew had actually seen them because they were always hidden inside a pair of gloves. He wore the thin, cotton variety often used in gardening or for work requiring some degree of dexterity. They reminded me of boxing gloves. And with his supercharged bearing, his clenched jaw, his eyes burning holes into the sidewalk before him, we were sure that Mr. Amos might turn into a boxer should we get too close. Growing up, I never watched him for any length of time without first scrambling to the other side of the street. And no matter where, or under which circumstances, I saw him, I never saw him for long, for Mr. Amos never tarried. He was always moving, always in a hurry, always focused on getting somewhere.

We never knew where.

Now, twenty years later, news of his death hits me like lightning as my boss, editor of the *Twin City News,* hands me a slip of paper with an address and tells me to hightail it over and get a story.

On the way, I phone my wife. "Did you hear Mr. Amos died?"

I pull up in front of the house and double-check, then triple-check, the address. I'm shocked at how close it is to the place where I grew up.

An old man wearing faded overalls greets me at the door and lets me inside, where it's warm and smoky. He tells me to call him Dave. I take a seat on a threadbare divan that's topped with a Florida State-colored, garnet and gold, afghan. There, in a photo above the TV, is Mr. Amos. His hair is thick and dark. He is smiling. He wears no gloves.

Dave calls off his little Chihuahua, which is also named Dave, and which is snarling at me. Then he begins to tell me what I've always wondered, what everyone in town has always wanted to know:

"David was my only son," he says. "He was one of the two best electricians in town. He wired this house here. Wired lots of houses around town. He was just a normal young man like anybody else. Then they killed Kennedy and that's when he flipped. We tried to help him, but he ended up going to the state hospital up in Chattahoochee. They gave him shock therapy, pills. He didn't respond to any of that. He was there three years before he ever set foot outside that fence. Eventually, he earned Trustee status and they'd let him out every day. He'd walk around town with his gloves and that brown paper bag. You remember his gloves, and that bag he carried? Once, not long after his mother passed away, I asked him what he had in that bag. I thought he was carrying around his lunch. He opened it and pulled out a couple coils of electrical wire and some fuses, a pair of wire cutters. He told me there was a house that needed rewiring, but he couldn't remember which one. I tried to tell him he was looking in the wrong place, but he wouldn't listen to me. After Kennedy died, he wouldn't listen to anyone."

In a Few Minutes I'll Be Gone

He felt badly asking her to leave, but he'd already told her she couldn't stay while he was out of town on business.

She'd been there three weeks, cooking his breakfast and dinner, cleaning his apartment every day, even though he never asked her to. He would come home in the evening and the place would smell like lemons and onions, and there would be two silverware settings on the table. She seemed to be able to tell, just from glancing at his face the moment he walked in the door, whether he wanted a beer or soda, or something else.

I'll miss having her around, he thought to himself as he sat at the table, sipping a soda and glancing at the kitchen cabinets. They seemed new, now that the dust and grease stains had been removed, now that they'd been coated in lemon polish. The pine veneer had a warm, honey color, which glowed in the late afternoon sunlight filtering in through the west window. A deep, warm pine in his own kitchen.

He'd met her on the Internet. He was trying to polish his Spanish. She was learning English and preparing for a trip to the United States, where she'd be visiting California, his state. Maybe he could show her some of the sights around Los Angeles; maybe she could help him with his Spanish.

There was never any formal agreement. Money never changed hands. But there had been an understanding, an arrangement, and up to this point it had worked fine.

But now he was leaving town and she simply couldn't stay.

"I will clean your apartment," she said, her back to him. She was balancing the basket of laundry on the edge of the washing machine. It was leaning against her body as she took the clothes and dropped them into the washer. "And do the wash."

What was it about doing the laundry that seemed to fascinate her? Was this her notion of love? Or was it the machines, themselves? The idea that they could take something dirty and make it clean and new? He'd asked her once, the time he'd found her with the dryer door cracked open as she peeked inside at the tumbling load. She'd responded by giggling and slipping in another sheet of fabric softener.

"I'd let you stay here, but like I said, it's a violation of my lease agreement. Besides, your visa's expiring."

She took the clean clothes out of the dryer, dropped them into the basket and, without looking at him, carried them to the table where he was sitting. The first item she picked up was one of his new work shirts. At least he thought it was one of his new work shirts; it was sugar-white, with the company logo on front. But there was something different about it. She shook out the wrinkles and held it up, her head tilted to one side.

Now he realized what it was. He pinched his bottom lip between his teeth and leaned back in his chair. She held the shirt out in front of him, her forehead scrunched. "I must have left it in too long."

"Don't worry about it," he said.

"Are you angry?"

"No," he said. "It doesn't matter."

"Please don't be angry with me."

"I'm not angry," he said, running his hand across the back of his neck and pulling, massaging the muscles. Finally, he sat up in his chair. "Look. I'll take you to the airport. I'll even pay for a motel if you need somewhere to stay before you go back. But I'm leaving in a little while and you can't be here when I'm gone."

There. It was done. He felt cruel, but relieved.

"Let me call, Luisa," she said.

"Go ahead," he said, thankful she had a friend. Luisa had traveled with her to the U.S. and was staying out in Riverside. Maybe she could stay with Luisa until they went back.

They talked for several minutes, her voice soft and reticent. She sat in the living room, on the edge of the sofa, while he leaned back in his chair at the kitchen table, looking again at the cabinets and their pine veneer glowing in the late afternoon sun. His soda can was empty now and he pushed it away.

She hung up the phone and sat there looking down at the floor.

"What did she say?" he said.

She didn't respond. She just sat there, elbows on her knees, hands clasped together.

He walked into the kitchen, dropped the empty can in the trash, and grabbed a beer from the refrigerator. He cracked it open and took a long drink. "Want a beer?" he said.

Then he heard the dryer start.

When he walked into the living room, she was gone. He looked in the bedroom, the bathroom, and out on the front stoop. Where was she?

Now the dryer began shaking. There was a heavy thud, then another. He opened the door and found her inside, her body contorted and spinning, and smelling of fabric softener, warm and fresh and new. "What are you doing?" he said. "Come out of there!"

But the door had already snapped shut and the drying cycle resumed, the thrashing and vibrating gradually diminishing until at last the machine spun smoothly, steadily, softly.

Droning

His wife, Sharon, is away more often now, her reserve unit keeping her a week or more at a time in preparation for its upcoming deployment to Fallujah. And after three or four days of making lunches and driving the kids to school, dragging himself to work and back home, and then dinner and homework and baths and teeth brushing and, finally, bedtime, Larry begins to feel hollow and insubstantial, like he might float away with the breeze, drift off into the clouds, into irrelevancy. Nights are the worst. Isolation rings so loudly in his ears that at times it seems they may burst. He turns the television on and invariably dials up alcohol to chase away the monotony of these one-sided conversations. Sometimes, he tells himself he should be the one deploying to the Middle East. More often, it's another voice he hears welling up from the basement of his mind, a voice that won't be silenced, that won't be washed away with the beer, telling him the kids have to be up by seven-thirty, that school starts at eight-thirty, that Lucy Jane, his youngest, prefers peanut-butter crackers in her lunch, that the kids need to be at school no later than eight-twenty, that he should take the left carpool lane because it's quicker... Then his usual response: *I've got it. Everything will be fine.*

It's Friday and after a long, dry week at the office, Larry stops off at the Git-n-Go for a twelve-pack. Back in his car, he darts across the street to the Army-Navy Surplus he's been itching to explore, the tripwire entry triggering the cowbell on the door, which clatters as he enters to an explosion of rubber and canvas, the somber sight of leather combat boots lined up in row after pointless row as if filled with the cold feet of dozens of attention-standing Sharons of different sizes, and yet of a singular, stony disposition, one indifferent to the tip of his index finger tapping, flicking, touching toe after toe as he examines the boots like some overzealous lieutenant inspecting his troops, one whom, in the absence of any discernible discrepancies, makes the same banal remarks to each soldier.

He spreads a formation of Triscuit crackers on a cookie sheet, tops them with spaghetti sauce and cheese, and places them into the warm oven. Five minutes later, when the cheese is bubbly, he serves them. "Hold on," he says as the kids hover over the tray. "Let them cool."

Lucy Jane, the eight-year-old, shakes her head and says, "This isn't how Mom makes pizza."

His boss has been talking for the better part of an hour. The company's value proposition. Its competitive advantage and position statement. The need to diversify. Etc., etc., etc. Sitting in the reclining leather chair, directly across the conference table from Katie, his bony-kneed colleague from sales, Larry's mind is like a static-filled radio cycling through the same dozen or so stations as it pulls in disparate frequencies, conflicting signals that crackle and flash momentarily before fading into obscurity: the e-mail he received this morning from Helen Krupps, his son's math teacher, who said Cam has missed turning in several homework assignments this week; the feasibility study he's been working on; sex with Sharon; the presentation he'll give to the executive committee two Mondays from now; the thought of sex with Katie; the overtime he'll have to put in to finish the presentation, now two weeks overdue; groceries he still needs to buy; the nagging feeling that his car might break down if he doesn't get it serviced; (groceries!); Sharon's voice: *I didn't ask for this war* (and his typical reply: "I didn't either!"); the thought of kissing Katie's bony knees…

The gadget on the surplus store's counter is shaped like a black question mark. It has three propellers and a remote-control unit with a full-color screen. "What's this?" Larry says, feeling as if he's been teleported back to his favorite toy store from childhood.

The Vietnam-era shopkeeper snuffs out his cigarette and flips his gray ponytail over his shoulder. The look on his face says he's explained the same thing to the last ten customers who asked about it, but at great pain and inconvenience, he'll do it again. "It's a bitchin' new toy," he says in a gravelly voice. "They call it the Phantom, but the name doesn't make a damn bit of difference. This is what's important," he says, pointing to the list of features. "Twenty minute flying time. Check," he says. "Sixteen megapixel camera for stills, check, and videos, check," he says. "And this is the best thing," he says. "You can watch everything right here on the remote, in real time," he says. "Check."

"Do you need a license for something like this?" Larry asks.

"It's like Dodge City out there, dude," the shopkeeper says as he inverts his cigarette pack and taps out a smoke, "before all the damned tourists showed up." He jams the cig into his lips, lights, inhales, squints, then lets loose with a long, smooth stream of smoke. "Just stay away from the airport with it and you'll be fine."

Sometimes, late of an evening, Sharon calls and he hears the contentment and tripod-steady purpose in her voice and he's both envious and frustrated. "So what do they have you doing?" he says.

"Same stuff," she says. "How are my babies?"

"They're fine," he says. "Sleeping." Then, "I miss you."

"Miss you too," she says.

"So when do you think you might be home?"

"Can't say," she says. "And even if I knew, you know I can't tell you on this unsecured line."

"Right," he says. "I know. I knew that."

"They're calling all the shots here, Hon," she says. "I'm just doing what I have to do and you're going to have to do the same. You know?"

"Yeah," he says as he imagines the afternoon heat weighing on Sharon, the sun's sharp rays carving crow's feet around her eyes, signs of her exposure, her commitment, scars she'll carry the rest of her life, which will remind both of them of her sacrifice. "I know," he says.

After the kids are in bed, he settles into the recliner, beer can in hand, and watches news coverage of the ongoing military operations in southwest Asia. The helicopters fascinate him, especially the Marine Corps' Super Cobra with its protruding twenty-millimeter cannon, which reminds him of the hornet he'd once encountered as a child. It descended on him from the rafters in his parents' garage, swirling, buzzing, causing Larry to flee in terror, screaming, swatting, although the hornet never stung him. Still, thinking about it now makes him sweat.

Gradually, his breathing accelerates along with his rate of consumption until, at some point, anxiety parachutes into the room and he finds himself worrying for Sharon, for her safety, while fighting the guilt that tends to pin him down and fire on him right there in his own living room nearly every night, volleys of incendiary thoughts lobbing back and forth in his mind: *What if? What if?* And, occasionally, that familiar voice: *You should be the one...*

It's the television that awakens him. When he opens his eyes, it's as if he's dreaming. Yellow, blue, and red lights converge on the wall beside the recliner, animated, animating. Cartoons, he realizes. He watches for a few seconds before a noise in the kitchen startles him. Cam and Lucy Jane are eating cereal at the kitchen table.

"You all want some juice with that?" Larry says, walking into the kitchen, feeling dizzy and disoriented, desperate for coffee, wondering if he should call in sick today.

"Dad, can we walk to school?" Cam asks. "It's not very far, and Kevin and Eric get to walk. Lots of kids walk," he says. "I'll watch Lucy Jane and make sure she gets there okay."

Larry looks at his daughter, who surprises him by saying, "Come on, Dad. Let us walk."

He waits until the kids are two houses down the sidewalk before sending up the Phantom. Then, from the recliner in the living room, he watches the procession of backpack-toting children ambling along the walkway like a column of colorful ants. Now a couple cars come into view on the screen, followed by a school bus, which from three hundred feet in the sky looks a bit like a yellow landing strip. There's a blip on the screen as something shoots by. A bird? Another drone? He descends for a better view and spots a woman leaving her house. He hovers above her as she walks to her car, opens the door and gets in.

Then his phone rings. It's Sharon.

"I wanted to say hi to the kids real quick," she says.

"You just missed them," Larry says as he leans back in the recliner. He extends the footrest, telling himself he's going to take a sick day. "They were up early this morning."

71

"Wish I'd called earlier. I'll try to call tonight," she says. "How's everything going?"

"Fine," he says, cradling the phone on his shoulder, eyes focused on the remote in his hands. "Everything's fine."

It Comes with the Territory

It's still dark when Mom wakes me, the sky outside my window black with the new moon. I sit up in bed, feeling the gravitational pull of the incoming tide as it floods the shallow sand flats just down the road, inundating my body, lifting the bow of my nose and gently rolling out from beneath my heels as I brush my teeth, pull a T-shirt over my head, slather sunscreen on my neck and arms.

In the kitchen, Mom hands me a piece of peanut-butter toast. She's made coffee even though Dad was the only one who drank it. Since he's been gone, I've been trying to like it. I pour some into a mug and top it off with milk and sugar. It's not bad like this. I think Mom just likes the smell of it in the kitchen. Reminds her of Dad.

"High tide's at nine-fifteen this morning," Mom says, turning the volume down on the marine radio in her hand. This is how she used to communicate with Dad when he was miles offshore with his clients, fishing. He died three months ago. Lung cancer. Mom still listens to the guides chattering about the weather, about who's catching what. Sometimes she'll say their names, laugh and shake her head. "There's Crusty Rusty," she'll say, talking about the cantankerous old guide who berates his clients when they lose a fish. Or, "There's Four-and-a-Half Frank," the captain who lost part of his first finger to a bull shark. All the captains have scars of some sort. My dad had puncture marks all over his arms and neck from his clients hooking him. It's part of being a fisherman.

Once, I caught Mom with the radio in her hand and tears streaming down her cheeks, and I knew they must have mentioned Dad's name, or maybe the name of the captain who bought his old boat. Or maybe she was thinking of the bank note she'd just paid off and the fact that there wasn't much left. Dad had no life insurance. Now, watching me eat, her face is stoic and sober, like the morning. "Water should be moving pretty good right now," she says.

"The bite's on," I say, gulping my coffee, choking down the thick toast.

"Think Flip will let you go out with him today?"

"He said if he has a full-day charter he might have room for me."

"You be careful out there," Mom says, patting my hand. "I know you're a big fisherman, but you're still my boy."

"I'm not a boy anymore, Mom. I can fish as well as anyone."

"I know you can. Your daddy taught you well," she says. "I packed you sardines in your lunch. You said you were tired of sandwiches."

"Thanks, Mom."

The air is cool as I pedal along the edge of the highway, thoughts of a day at sea pulling me along like the tide, the same tide that courses through my veins, that concentrates the fish, that dictates life here in the Florida Keys. Fishing is in my blood and it's nearly all I think about. I've been on boats with my dad since I could walk. I'm only fourteen, but I can tie a Bimini twist and rig a sailfish spread just like he taught me. I've been coming down here every day since he passed away, hoping one of the captains needs a mate, hoping today's the day I'll get to show the world I know how to catch fish.

Bugs are still buzzing around the dock lights when I arrive at the marina. Men wearing shorts and flip-flops, caps on their heads and sunglasses hanging from neck lanyards, crowd around the front of the store, sipping coffee or massaging sunscreen into their skin. Bud, the owner of the marina, is taking orders for bait: squid, pilchards, mullet, shrimp. I love marinas, especially this one, which is where Dad used to keep his boat. You come down here early in the morning and everyone's happy and slapping each other on the back, talking about the fish they're going to catch. Some just want to have fun, but for others fishing is more important. It's a way of life.

I lean my bike against the storefront, beside the ice machine, and take my lunch down to the docks where men are moving back and forth, carrying rods and reels, boxes of tackle and bait. I can tell what they're fishing for by the kind of gear they're carrying. Those with giant reels are going after marlin or tuna. The fly fishermen are here to chase tarpon on the flats. That's the fish I know best, though it's hard to convince most adults that a fourteen-year old knows how to get these giants to bite.

Down the dock, at slip 47, I see Flip welcoming a

couple sports onto his boat. I head over and say hello.

"Morning, Mark," he says, resting his bare foot on the gunwale. Around his eyes, and looking like a white mask, is a tan line from his sunglasses, which now hang from his neck. "Wish I could take you out today, but they only booked me for half a day."

That's Flip for you. Non-committal. Unwilling to take a chance. Polite, but full of excuses. A lot of people think that's why he's not married.

"No problem," I say, feeling my heart dropping through the depths like an anchor.

"Why don't you let Bud know you're looking for work," he says. "He might know of something."

"Sure," I say. Flip's a nice guy, but he's just letting me down easy. Cash is tight in this economy. Guides aren't running as many charters as they used to and there's not much demand for mates.

Still, the sting of rejection is overwhelming. Since Dad's been gone, I find myself doing weird things. Like giving myself a hashmark tattoo with a hot fork. Like piercing my left ear with a barbless fish hook. Today, I rake my knuckles across a stack of cinderblocks as I head back up the dock.

I take a seat on the picnic table in front of the marina store, where I watch men tote their gear from the parking lot to the boats. I watch these same boats pull away from the docks and head out to sea, each one destined for its own adventure. For me, it's another lost summer day with no work, stuck here on shore.

A few minutes later, I spot Bud and approach him. "Just wanted to let you know I'm still available, if you know of any of the captains looking for a mate," I tell him.

Bud's an intimidating guy. He was in Vietnam and he doesn't like crowds or loud noises. Once, I saw him chew a man out just for dropping a box of frozen bait.

"Thank you, Mark," he says. There's a tattoo of a bulldog on his knotty right bicep, beneath which are the letters USMC. "You're getting to be pretty big. Another year or two and I'm sure we can get you out on one of these boats."

"I can take a Penn Senator apart and put it back together in less than fifteen minutes. My dad taught me."

He grabs a bucket off the bait tank and begins filling it with live shrimp. "Your daddy loved those Penns, didn't he? How old are you, Mark?"

"Fourteen."

"Tell you what. Come see me when you're sixteen and we'll talk," he says.

From the way he says it, I know the conversation is over and I get that feeling in my stomach like I've swallowed a pound of lead sinkers. It's the feeling of rejection and it makes me crazy, especially when I know I can do the job.

I get back on my bike and head over to Robbie's Marina, just down the highway, where there's always a group of tourists feeding the resident tarpon off the docks. Surprisingly, there's no one around this morning, so I walk down to the dock and watch these prehistoric-looking fish swimming through the clear, shallow water. Their goggle eyes look up at me, having been conditioned to expect food. Some of these tarpon are bigger than me, and older. Their silver scales are like mirrors, reflecting the sand as they swim by or hover just beneath the surface, watching my every move, waiting.

I open my lunch, take out the tin of sardines Mom packed and twist it open. Then I grab one of the oily fish by the tail and hold it out over the water, watching as the tarpon move into position beneath my hand. Drops of oil fall from the sardine, landing on the water with a gentle *plop,* then dissipating.

I've wrestled fish bigger than these hundred-pound tarpon, but Bud doesn't know this. He probably thinks I'd get seasick out there.

I flick the sardine and one of the tarpon explodes from the water, launching its six feet of silver-scaled muscle straight up into the air, giant gill rakers rattling, its cavernous mouth opening and engulfing my hand. I should let go of the bait now, but I've got something to prove to Bud, to Flip, to everyone.

My brain fires orders to my arm: *Pull back! Pull back!* But I manage to resist and brace myself against a pier as the tarpon clamps his cinderblock mouth around my hand. For a moment the tarpon and me are eye-to-eye, two anglers shaking hands, a tiny piece of bait connecting us to another world. Then, as gravity pulls the fish back into the water, I feel his gritty teeth, themselves microscopic fish hooks, abrading my skin.

Blood streams down my fingers and drips into the water where moments ago sardine oil had been. They think I'm too young to work the boats, to go out into the bluewater. But I'm a fisherman and I've got the scars to prove it.

I take another sardine from the tin and hold it out over the water.

Lean Methodology

The layoffs began right after the company was sold. The new owners cut staff from accounting and sales; they closed the research department. My friend, Sal, lost his job.

A few weeks ago, they brought in Howard, this mass of metal with bulbous black lenses and twinkling diodes, warning-label tattoos: *Caution! Unit may malfunction in temperatures above 90° F!*

Howard, they say, is here to help us be more data-driven and efficient. Really, I think the new owners are trying to send a message: Howard doesn't call in sick. Howard doesn't need health benefits or pay raises. Howard requires so little, but gives so much.

Too much, if you ask me. All it does is spit out data and take up space. Yesterday, I found it in my office. Today it's in my boardroom seat.

I turn to Laura, the senior manager, who sits at the head of the table. "All these seats and it has to take mine?" I say. "I've been sitting here for twelve years."

The LEDs on Howard's face are blinking. Finally, it says, "Gross revenues are down twelve percent from this time last year."

Now there's laughter, knee slapping around the table. Laura seems particularly amused, but she's used to these mindless computers. She has one at home that cleans her floors.

"He doesn't understand the concept of having a favorite," she says.

"You mean *it*," I say, looking again at Howard, whose head swivels toward me as I take a seat. I refuse to refer to it as a "he," even though it wears a man's suit, a perfectly fitted man's suit, which public affairs had specially made.

"We're glad you're here," Laura says. "You can be the tiebreaker."

"What's the tie?" I say.

"The tie industry is flourishing this year," Howard says, its LEDs flashing green and black. "Sales of men's bow ties are up forty percent over last year."

Across the table, Ralph, who manages accounting, shakes his head. Laura leans over and pats Howard on the shoulder.

"It can't feel that," I say. "It's not even on the margins of being human, so that means nothing."

"Gross margins have dropped to five percent this quarter," Howard says, its neck swivel squeaking as it pans its head around the table. "This is unsustainable."

"He's right," Laura says. "That's why Al wants us to reduce our FTE count. *Again.* So, do we lay off three from IT, or marketing?"

"Why is it up to me? I don't want to make that decision," I say.

"It's up to all of us, and we've all voted. Even Howard weighed in," Laura says as she pulls a sweater over her shoulders, crosses her arms.

"It gets a vote?"

"Yes, and now you get to be the tiebreaker."

Everyone looks at me as I consider this.

"Allison in marketing just had a baby," I say. "She needs health insurance. You can't lay her off. Then you have Pete, who's been here forever. He's only a few years away from retirement. Are we that cold and heartless?"

"It's just business," Laura says. "It's not personal."

"It is if you're the one getting canned," I say.

Just then, Al, our president, walks into the meeting. "It's cold in here. What's the temperature?"

Ralph stands from the table. "I'll check the thermometer."

"I think it's our friend, Howard," Laura says. "He's in rare form today."

"He's a whole new prototype," Al says. "New operating system and everything. Does the work of an entire research department."

I glare at Howard, grit my teeth.

"No wonder," Ralph says. "Temperature's on sixty-nine. I'll turn it up."

Howard's face twinkles yellow-orange. "A temperature range of sixty-five to seventy-five degrees Fahrenheit is optimal for our products," it says.

Laura looks at Howard and grins. "Howard, have you been toying with the temperature again?"

Once again, the robot's face twinkles yellow-orange. "A temperature range of sixty-five to seventy-five degrees Fahrenheit is optimal for our products."

"He's exactly right. Guess the rest of us can wear a jacket," Al says. Then, to everyone: "So, do we have a decision? We need to get this done by close of business today."

"We're talking about it," Laura says. "It's a tough decision because Allison just had her baby, but Pete's so close to retirement."

Al shakes his head. "You're missing the point," he says. "I want you to stop thinking about people and start thinking like managers."

Silence.

"Look," Al says, pointing to Howard. "Use him as an example. Just the facts and figures. This isn't about people. It's all about the data. Good data drives revenues."

The LEDs on Howard's face are blinking. "Gross revenues are down twelve percent from this time last year."

"That's exactly right," Al says, moving to the door. "I need your decision ASAP."

After he's gone, Laura says, "Marketing's overstaffed, so you know my vote."

Ralph leans back in his chair. "I agree."

"Marketing," Regina says.

"The marketing department exceeded its budget by twenty percent last quarter," Howard says.

"We know Howard's vote," Laura says. Then to me, "So what about you?"

"I think we need to take our time and think about this," I say. "These are people's lives we're messing with. This isn't just about labor costs."

"Currently, fifty percent of the marketing budget is allocated to labor costs," Howard says. "This is unsustainable."

"Doesn't this thing ever stop talking?" I say.

"Only if we do," Laura says. "He's programmed that way."

I shake my head and loosen my tie. "Maybe we should take a break."

"I could use a bathroom break," Regina says.

"All right," Laura says. "Be back here in ten minutes."

"We offer a ten-year warranty on our products," Howard says, the LEDs on his face flashing. "Your satisfaction is guaranteed."

We stand and file out of the boardroom, leaving Howard alone at the table. On the way out the door, I crank the thermometer to ninety-five.

Pathogen

Headline: *Thirteen hospitalized after exposure to city air!*

"Stay indoors!" authorities warned.

"Add a third shift!" the carmaker said. "We can be number one again!"

Threats Include Habitat Loss
and Degradation

Spring 2010

Plaquemines Parish, Louisiana

His boat docked, his crew at home in their beds, sleeping in for the twelfth consecutive morning, his wife standing beside him on the pier, a shrimp fisherman fields questions from the growing legion of news reporters arriving to cover the Deepwater Horizon disaster, and which each day roves the local beaches like a school of hungry fish, lured by the scent of petroleum, poised for the feeding frenzy that'll sustain viewing audiences for weeks:

"How is this gonna impact my season?" the shrimper says, repeating a reporter's question. He thinks about it, then says, "I'd say my season's over. And probably my career." His wife takes his hand and squeezes. "Anybody want to buy a forty-foot shrimp trawler?"

Pensacola, Florida

Residents monitor the growing oil slick through a local newspaper's headlines:

May 6: *Scientists Speculate West Florida Safe from Oil.*

Pass Christian, Mississippi

A restaurant owner/chef/server to a customer:

"We just reopened last year. The old place blew away in the hurricane in 2005," she says. "You need more shrimp, hon? Yes, they're fresh. We use Carolina shrimp, delivered here every Tuesday."

Gulf Shores, Alabama

A paid spokesman, sunglasses on, his pant legs rolled up and slogging through the sand, pipes to the TV camera:

"Come on down to the Alabama Gulf Coast! The sky's just as blue as always!"

Pensacola, Florida

May 11: *Dead Dolphins Discovered in Gulf!*

Mobile, Alabama

A family spurting along the Jubilee Parkway over Mobile Bay en route to an East Coast vacation:

"Do you smell that?" the husband says to his wife as he turns off the vent fan.

The wife, staring out the window, says: "There aren't even any fishermen out in the bay."

Biloxi, Mississippi

A local high-school English teacher has an op-ed published in *The New York Times.*

"Not since the publication of Ernest Hemingway's 'The Killers' has America felt such a sense of impending doom," her editorial begins. "But if the BP oil disaster is the left hook that's put the Gulf Coast on its heels, the inevitable, knockout blow will most certainly be the growing realization that there's not a damn thing we can do about it!"

Destin, Florida

A tourism official responding to reports that tar balls are washing onto Alabama beaches:

"There's no oil on *our* beaches," he gushes to the reporter. Then, to the camera: "Come on down!"

Panama City Beach, Florida

A fishing guide, whose client has just called to cancel his morning trip:

"Snapper live on the bottom," he says. "Even if you don't want to eat them, they're still fun to catch," he says. "Or maybe you like bass fishing better. I got a lake full of lunkers. It's nowhere near the coast."

Pensacola, Florida

May 20: *Oil Spotted Thirty Miles Offshore!*

Carrabelle, Florida

At a barbeque stand on the edge of town, two customers waiting in line strike up a conversation:

"I've never seen anything like it," says an old man, a local. "They say it's going to turn our water black and kill all our fish. A dead zone, they call it, just like the one at the mouth of the Mississippi River over there," he says. "Can't nothing live in a dead zone."

The other man, an engineer from a petroleum company, who's been sent to monitor the local beaches, says, "The bacteria in the water will eat the oil. That's not a problem."

"What about everything that eats the bacteria?" says the old man.

Pensacola, Florida
May 30: *Oil is at Our Doorstep!*

Autumn 2014

Distribution list: nationwide
An e-mail message sent by the Ocean Trust:
Ever since the BP disaster in the Gulf of Mexico four years ago, we've been asking: Where did all the oil go? Now we know. A recent report tells us there's a blanket of oil the size of New Jersey that's fouled the bottom of the Gulf. We need your help!

Plaquemines Parish, Louisiana
A former shrimp fisherman, remembering his days at sea with his crew, and growing restless from sitting at home and watching CNN, talks to the television, the sofa, his otherwise empty home:

"With gas prices going down, makes me wish I had my old boat back. You know?" he says. "Only there's nothing left to catch around here anymore. I wish you'd come back."

Out on the Edge of the World

We hadn't been in the Oklahoma Territory long. Maybe two weeks. My father and the old man who was helping us with the dugout shelter had just sat down to dinner at the edge of the creek where the trees offered some respite from the wind. My mother had made a stew with the pheasant my father shot the day before, and he sat there eating while the old man, who had long, white chin whiskers and a Colt revolver on his hip, slurped coffee from a saucer and told stories about fighting the Cheyenne on this same land. I wanted to ask where the Indians had gone, but my brother, Clyde, and me weren't allowed to disturb the men. So I just listened and after a while the old man said something that got my attention. "They wanted them out," he said, "so they came through here and killed all their buffalo."

My mother was busy making biscuit dough, so Clyde and me slipped into the trees and headed down the dry creek bed, following my tracks from the day before.

"Where you taking me?"

"Just follow me," I said.

Clyde was quiet and bookish, and when we weren't helping my father with some chore, he was content to just sit around and read. Not me. Out there on those plains I felt like I was on the edge of the world, like I was on an adventure. It was so different from Ohio. The land was open and rolling, and you could see the wind rippling the grass for a good piece in any direction. The sun shined every day. There were varmints everywhere. At night, you could listen to coyotes yipping while you looked up at all those stars glittering like new coins.

We walked for a good piece, Clyde and me, and eventually climbed out of the creek bed and hightailed it up a long, low ridge–downwind, of course. I'd learned that from the old man.

"What is it?" Clyde said.

I told him to take off his hat and keep quiet.

We slipped through grass nearly as tall as we were. Then, near the top, we got on our bellies and pulled ourselves up to the edge where we looked down into an enormous valley of green as the wind rustled the grass and field larks sang all around us. At the bottom was a watering hole, wind-rippled and looking like a broken mirror, shattered pieces reflecting the blue sky. I pointed to the five brown masses just beyond. They were oblong-shaped with bulging humps on one side, tapering into narrow waists. Every now and then the beasts would move a few paces and drop their heads to the ground. I could see their tails twitching and swatting flies.

"Buffalo!" Clyde whispered. "Reckon the hunters didn't get them all."

"That there's probably the last of them," I said. "But it's still not enough."

Cold

Walking into the pet store, he spots her, standing by the rack of leashes and wearing those tight jeans with the wild stitching along the seams.

She looks over and he wishes he hadn't stopped.

He tilts his head, mouths a greeting he knows she can't hear, and heads off in the opposite direction. Angling now toward the far side of the store, he passes through birds, cats, and finally into reptiles where his reflection drifts like smoke over the terrariums of lizards, turtles, and near the end of the corridor, a black snake. He studies the snake, coiled and motionless in the corner of the terrarium. Save for its cold black eye, watching him, the reptile might be dead. Wishbone shivers and steps back from the glass.

A voice at the opposite end of the aisle rattles him: "Wishbone, you don't even *like* snakes!"

I *might* like snakes, he thinks to himself. I *might* like lots of things I haven't told you about.

Finally, he says, "I'm just looking."

"You just looking at me, too! You just walk by like you don't even know me!"

"I said '*What up*'?"

"Don't stand there like you don't know what I'm talking about!"

"You don't have to yell," he says, looking over his shoulder.

"This ain't yelling," she says. "I can yell if you *want* me to!"

"Man, just chill. What do you want me to say?"

After a pause, she says, "My *name*. Next time you see me."

"All right," he says.

"People like it when you remember their name. It's a form of respect. It shows you care."

The snake flicks its tongue and again Wishbone inches back from the terrarium, into the middle of the aisle. "All right then," he says to the girl. He jams a hand into his pocket, feels his phone's rubber bumper. For a second, he takes his mind off the girl standing in front of him–Jackie is her name. Or is it Jacquelyn?–and thinks of another.

She sighs heavily, shifting her weight to the opposite leg. Then she reaches into her purse and removes a tube of lipstick, which she twists open and applies. It's purple. "You still got my number in your phone?"

"Yeah."

She smacks her lips together, drops the tube back into her purse. "What name you got it under?"

"It's in there," he says, trying to remember if it's Jackie or Jacquelyn. He glances to his left and notices their reflection in a mirror. Across the bottom are these words: *Objects in mirror are closer than they appear.*

"Under what name?" she says.

Suddenly, he hears Marvin Gaye singing, feels his phone buzzing in his pocket. "Hello," he says.

"All I ask for is a little respect!" says the girl standing at the end of the aisle. She shakes her head, her eyes narrowed and locked onto his. "A little respect that you can't seem to give. You won't even *say my name!*"

With the phone to his ear, he watches the girl in front of him, but he can't hear what she's saying.

"Wishbone!" says the girl at the end of the aisle, slinging her purse over her shoulder. "I'm done trying to be nice to you!"

The voice from the phone reverberates through his body like a dull vibration even as the girl in front of him continues shouting. He can't understand what she's saying, this girl. Is she Jackie? Jacquelyn? He still can't remember. She's yelling so loudly that now he can't understand what the girl on the phone is telling him. It's sensory overload. It's overwhelming. He'd like to slip into one of these terrariums, curl up in the sawdust and hide.

The girl in front of him shakes her head. "You don't appreciate anything! Cold as hell!"

After she's gone, he tells the girl on the phone he has to go. She's still talking when he ends the call and slides the phone back into his pocket.

He looks again at the snake in the terrarium, coiled and motionless, its gleaming black eye watching his every move. Again it flicks its tongue. Goose bumps pimple his arms.

Instead of walking straight ahead, through reptiles, as before, he turns and goes the other way. When he comes to the dog-food section, he stops and lingers, perusing the many different offerings. Finally, he grabs a blue bag and heads off to the register to pay.

In the parking lot, the afternoon heat radiates up from the asphalt, warming him. He feels better already. Until he reaches his car.

There, on the windshield, *Joyce* is written in purple cursive script, over and over and over. The name also appears, in white, on his blue hood. He drags his finger through one of the letters, but it doesn't smear. Now he traces the name with his finger, knowing he'll never get it out.

To Better Serve You

KEEN KLIENT
Hi, I need a quote on a ride. Would you please tell me your rates? Thx, Tara

KEEN KLIENT KARE
Kongratulations! You've just kontacted KEEN KARS (www.keenkars.com), home of the keenest, greenest rides, koast to koast! We're happy to assist you, Tara. May we have your city, please? (To find out more about KEEN KARS, klick here!)

KEEN KLIENT
Columbus

KEEN KLIENT KARE
Albuquerque is a wonderful city!

KEEN KLIENT
COLUMBUS!

KEEN KLIENT KARE
Kolumbus is a wonderful city!
Here are our rates for Kolumbus:

- Base rate: $2.50. Then add:
- $0.25 per minute, plus
- $2.50 per KEEN KILOMETER
  (What's a KEEN KILOMETER? Klick here!)
  Minimum fare: $10.00
  Cancellation fee: $9.99

KEEN KLIENT
So, could you give me the total fare for this ride?
LEAVING: 11492 14th Street NE
ARRIVING: 22 Southbound Way

KEEN KLIENT KARE
Absolutely!

KEEN KLIENT
Thank you.

*KOMPUTING… KOMPUTING… KOMPUTING…
KOMPUTING…KOMPUTING*

KEEN KLIENT KARE
Tara, we'll have your fare shortly. In the meantime, please
konsider some of our KEEN KUSTOMIZATIONS–options to
help you make the most of your ride. (To learn more about
KEEN KUSTOMIZATIONS, klick here!)

KEEN KLIENT
I just need a ride. What kind of options?

KEEN KLIENT KARE
Here are some of our most popular:

- X-TRA KLEEN RIDE (Kar will arrive washed,
  waxed, and smelling of KEEN's KUSTOM
  KOKONUT air freshener.)
- HI-PERFORMANCE RIDE (Money buys speed.)
- KEEN KICKER PACKAGE (Those who enjoy loud,
  thumping bass love our KEEN KICKER, which kicks
  like a krazed kamel! It will leave you kraving more!)

• GUARANTEED KRASH-FREE RIDE (In the highly unlikely event of a kar krash, KEEN KARS will pay you!)

Don't forget that every fare includes komplimentary bottled water (not recommended with KEEN KICKER PACKAGE) and klimate kontrol.

Tara, would you be interested in any of these KEEN KUSTOMIZATIONS? (To learn more about KEEN KUSTOMIZATIONS, klick here!)

KEEN KLIENT
No. Just the total fare.

KEEN KLIENT KARE
Absolutely!

KOMPUTING… KOMPUTING… KOMPUTING… KOMPUTING…KOMPUTING

KEEN KLIENT KARE
Tara, if you haven't already done so, now would be a great time to download our KEEN KARS app! It allows you to reserve and kustomize a ride anytime and anyplace that's konvenient for you. Whether you need a lift to the office kubicle, or your komfortable krib, the KEEN KARS app has you kovered! (Download the KEEN KARS app by klicking here!)

KEEN KLIENT
Just need the fare, please.

KEEN KLIENT KARE
Absolutely!

*KOMPUTING… KOMPUTING… KOMPUTING…
KOMPUTING…KOMPUTING*

KEEN KLIENT KARE
Tara, your fare is $12.50. This fare includes no kustomizations and is based on a 5-karat klient rating. We're happy to reserve this ride for you. We accept MasterCard, Visa, or the KEEN KREDIT KARD, which entitles you to a 1.5 % discount and komplimentary air freshener on your next ride with KEEN KARS. (Accent your wallet with the KEEN KREDIT KARD. Apply today!) (To find out more about KEEN KARS, klick here!)

KEEN KLIENT
Wait. My rating is only 3.5 karats.

KEEN KLIENT KARE
Oh, dear. Tara, we may still be able to serve you, but at an additional kost. Please wait while we check your reviews.

Unreasonable request for bathroom break? Reviewed by Oscar.

KEEN KLIENT
Oh, that. We were sitting in a traffic jam for, like, two hours.

KEEN KLIENT KARE
Backseat driver? Reviewed by Tarek.

KEEN KLIENT

They never listen to me! So I end up having to repeat myself. Then they pretend to speak only Swahili or German. Scroll down and you'll see some of my good reviews. Keep reading.

KEEN KLIENT KARE

Road rage? Reviewed by Anonymous.

KEEN KLIENT

The sonofabitch cut us off!

KEEN KLIENT KARE

For treatment of minor kuts and bruises, sprains and strains, and for all your flu-shot needs, visit the KEEN KARES Medical Klinik near you. (To find a KEEN KARES KLINIK in your city, klick here!)

KEEN KLIENT

I just need a ride!

KEEN KLIENT KARE

Tara, based on your 3.5-karat klient rating, KEEN KARS is unable to serve you at this time. We're sorry.

KEEN KLIENT

But I need a ride, and you put the taxi companies out of business with your Keen Karma program.

KEEN KLIENT KARE

We kould refer you to our high-risk division, but we must warn you the rates are kommensurate with your klient rating, which means they kould be kost-prohibitive for someone of your temperament. Or, we kould transfer you to KEEN KRATES, our new bike division. (What's a KEEN KRATE? Klick here.)

KEEN KLIENT

You're not getting me on a bike. I don't ride bikes.

KEEN KLIENT KARE

Tara, our records indicate you used to own a bike.
In 1993. We show your address at the time was
2109 Elm Avenue, Kolumbus.

KEEN KLIENT

I was 9 years old! Look: I don't ride bikes. It's too hot, anyway. But I guess I have no choice. Send me to your bike division.

KEEN KLIENT KARE

Tara, your aversion to bikes, and the heat, have lowered your klient rating to 3.3 karats, which means you no longer meet the minimum requirements for KEEN KRATES. We're sorry. (What's a KEEN KRATE? Klick here!)

KEEN KLIENT

This is so stupid! All I want is a ride! I have a job interview!

KEEN KLIENT KARE

Unemployed? Tara, your klient rating is now 2.5 karats. If it drops any lower, we'll be forced to terminate this KEEN KOMMUNIKATION.

KEEN KLIENT

Why can't I speak to a real person? Why doesn't your website list your phone number? Is talking with your customers directly too RISKY?

KEEN KLIENT KARE

Tara, reducing your risk of identity theft is a smart move. Protect your personal information by signing up for KEEN KOVERAGE, which allows you to purchase additional karats to improve your KEEN KLIENT rating while also entitling you to komplimentary air freshener on your next ride with KEEN KARS. (What is KEEN KOVERAGE? Klick here!) (Want to kick up your KEEN KLIENT rating? Klick here!) (To find out more about KEEN KARS, klick here!)

KEEN KLIENT

THIS IS RIDICULOUS!!! WHO'S IN CHARGE THERE??? IF ONLY THERE WERE ANOTHER OPTION HERE IN COLUMBUS, YOU'D BE OUT OF BUSINESS!!!

KEEN KLIENT KARE

Albuquerque is a wonderful city!

Lost

Fifteen years, his unruly, upstairs neighbor likes to remind him in those empty, uncertain hours of night, *is twenty percent of the average American male's lifespan! That'll throw a wheel out of balance!*

Of course, he knows this, can in fact still hear his lawyer arguing on his behalf, that time served is time he cannot replace. Taken from him. Gone.

Fifteen years! his neighbor points out, as if he's forgotten, as if he hasn't thought about it nearly every minute of every one of the ninety-nine days he's been on the outside. Which is why he keeps the radio on, morning, noon, and night. Silence is a rabble-rouser.

Although he was exonerated, his name cleared, he didn't get everything back. How could he? When he thinks about it like this, late at night, lying there in that fragmented apartment, trying to remember faces, names, numbers, and what the world looked like before, before, even the quarter-million-dollar settlement his lawyer negotiated for him seems inadequate, inconsequential. Unless… he can't be sure.

He heard disbelief's voice for so long that eventually it moved in with him and became his cellmate. Then one night his memory slipped through the bars and escaped, and suddenly he couldn't recall a time when he hadn't doubted, when he hadn't seen himself through the eyes of others. After all, if he'd needed any evidence, there he was, wearing orange shame, eating for sustenance rather than pleasure, with no use for a calendar. And yet he was innocent. That's what he always maintained. Innocent. That's what his lawyer had argued. Innocent.

Technicality: that's what everyone else said. Even after DNA evidence helped overturn his conviction. Even after the newspaper dedicated three column inches to setting the record straight. Everyone said it was just a technicality. Just a glitch in the system. A minor detail had set him free.

His lawyer said to ignore them, said to look forward, not back, said to get on with his life, that he's only thirty-five, that–if one could believe statistics, research–he'd probably live another thirty-five.

It's going on four months now and though disbelief packed up and went away he can still hear self-doubt stumbling around upstairs in the cruel, wicked hours of night, rattling him with its shackled footfalls, hurling antagonistic slurs–*fifteen years!*–as if it has nothing better to do than stay behind and torment him.

Other than groceries–just the basics; a learned behavior which has become habit; but then again his idea of eating well has always been getting *enough* to eat, hasn't it?–and batteries for the radio, which he buys in bulk, the only thing he's sprung for so far is a pair of reading glasses, faux tortoiseshell cheaters that multiply like rumors and which make him feel like an historian as he scans the residential listings at his local library, reveling in the room's wide-open space and the vague camaraderie of the other visitors as he scrolls through screens, scanning, the hairs on back of his neck bristling occasionally, his head jerking and twisting whenever someone approaches from behind, then the breathing techniques, deep breaths, and the counting and holding and waiting as he centers himself in the winter of his fuzzy, if familiar, discontent. And all the while he never stops searching for names that might help him fill that fifteen-year void. He tells himself that perhaps he can connect with someone he used to know, a friend or former co-worker from the car lot, which is now just a tire shop. Or maybe he has some family left, someone out there somewhere who can remind him who or what he used to be, who can substantiate that what he believes—what he *wants* to believe—is true, that his freedom is the product of something innate, something more than the minor technicality his upstairs neighbor insists. He has money now and he tells himself that he'd spend all of it to prove he is who he always said he was. And if he can't do this, he thinks, what's the point of going on? What use is money, even a quarter million, to a man who can't look at himself in the mirror, tell himself he's innocent, and really believe it?

First Monday

She said: *For a hope chest, I'd say it's a bargain.* He said: *I've been calling it a cedar chest.* She said: *What I mean is, you could get a lot more for it.* He said: *It's been used.* She said: *Don't I know it?* He said: *If you decide you want it, maybe we could work something out.* She said: *I bet we could.* He said: *I saw you when you came through earlier.* She said: *It's only been five days.* He said: *I was hoping you'd stop by.* She said: *I'm just looking.* He said: *That was my line.* She said: *Only it wasn't true, though, was it?* He said: *If you decide you want it, I can deliver it.* She said: *You sound desperate.* He said: *I don't have the space for it anymore, plus what am I going to put in it?* She said: *Is that really why you're getting rid of it?* He said: *Still looks good, though, doesn't it?* She said: *But it doesn't do anything for you, does it?* He said: *I guess you didn't take that job in Houston?* She said: *Don't ask.* He said: *I didn't see you at the gym last week.* She said: *I meant to tell you I went out and got that tattoo.* He said: *Did I tell you I traded my old Jeep for a pickup?* She said: *You didn't waste any time, did you?* He said: *I have covered parking now.* She said: *What's the best you can do?* He said: *I can bring it to you.* She said: *Not enough.* He said: *That's always been the problem.*

When the Levee Breaks

When they pushed off, the water was clear and shallow, and they could see the bottom beneath them, smooth and pebbly, and solid, as they glided through placid pools of passion and contentment. Gradually—some say inevitably—the river widened and deepened until one year they found themselves navigating at flood stage, a contingency they hadn't considered and one that exposed innate differences in their respective responses to danger. She wanted to pull for shore. He said they could ride it out, even as the tricky currents threatened to capsize them. Still rising, the muddy water, now of an unknown depth, submerged its secrets, concealing the sticky mud and logjams and other hazards which couldn't be seen but which waited to sink them just the same. He wondered if they could feel their way around these obstacles. She said by the time they felt them it would be too late. Then she said it was already too late and he panicked.

Sucked into currents they couldn't control, into vacuum-like eddies that swirled and churned, and disoriented them, and on through the straits of reconciliation, past love's last low-water bridge, itself inundated by a thousand cubic feet per second, they went over the falls, split up on the rocks below and, damaged—some say irreparably so—drifted apart.

Now parents, river guides, members of the clergy bring their children, clients, their parishioners, respectively, leading group trips planned months in advance, and often at great expense, to view the rocky plunge pool beneath the falls, which has been crashed upon by so many lost vessels that the boulders have broken down into rocks, which are being reduced to pebbles and are in danger of becoming gritty silt and disappearing altogether. Look what happens, they say, when we lose sight of the bottom, with no faith to buoy us. They point to the rapidly diminishing stones as their groups snap photos and gaze with wonder at the site of so much wreckage. Even the biggest boulders, they say, are reduced to nothing.

The Franchise

Guess how much my paychecks are. Take a guess. Nope. Way more than that. Nope. Nope. *Touchdown!* Yep. Every two weeks! Can you believe it? I know. You should see the place I bought. When you and Dad come up, you can have your own... No, not really. Because I spend all my time practicing or working out. We get Tuesdays off, but... I sold it. Had to. It's in my contract. No motorcycles and no convertibles. Yes. I'm saving most of it. I'm giving some away, too. My agent wants me to start a foundation. I know, but I had to get a place. No. I took that one back. I just have two now. Because I don't *have* a girlfriend. I don't know. I just haven't met anyone. When would I do that? It's not *that* big, I guess. I mean, it's *big*, but I could've bought... Because I liked *this* one. You ought to see the limestone entry. The front door is off this old castle from... I don't know. They said they were going to call. They really want you all to move up here. There's a place just around the corner from mine. You'd love... Doesn't matter. They're going to pay for it. Doesn't matter. They'll buy your old... Because they think I'm going to go out and get in trouble or something. I told them I'm twenty-three. I have a college degree. I can look after... She's nice. She comes over every day and cleans. Then there's Susan. She's about your age. Nice lady. Cooks all my meals, unless I tell her I want to eat out. If I do, I call this guy and he arranges it. They bring me whatever I... No, I haven't been there. Maybe in the off season. Steak and eggs, usually. Or salmon. They want me to eat lots of protein and... I haven't been there either. Unless I'm going to the facility, I almost never leave the house. After the last time, they told me I needed a disguise. *Seriously!* I'm not wearing a disguise. I am who I am. I'm not going to pretend to be somebody... On Tuesdays? I sleep in, usually. Play video games. Sometimes I go out back and hit golf balls into the lake or... Everyone knows who I am. That's why. They'll mob me. Yesterday was the first day in *eleven days* that my name or photo wasn't in the paper. I know. It's fine. I can go out if I want. It's just, you know, I don't want to deal with it. And I'm not wearing a... I know. I know. Really, it's fine. You know. But sometimes I just want to go out for a milkshake or go shopping, and I have to call Roger, that's my bodyguard, and it's like, What's going on here? Who are you? And then... I did? Oh, I didn't mean to forget his birthday. I've just been... Well then tell me what he... Tell me what he wants and I'll send it to him. He'll get over it.

Wish You Were Here

"I wish Momma was here," I say, adjusting the straps over Garrett's ears, clicking the buckle into place.

"Because you don't know how to cook?" Garrett says.

"Yeah. That too." I take a few steps back, kneel, and raise the camera. "Look at me. Okay, smile." *Click-click.*

"Can we go now?"

"In a minute," I say. "Your mother's going to have a degree in two years, but she'll never know what this was like. I want to have some photos to show her."

"You know what to do if you see a car backing out, right? You stop. You pull the brake, like this." I squeeze the lever and the brake calipers clamp the rim, immobilizing it.

"I already know that," Garrett says, pushing my hand away.

"How's your seat? Do we need to adjust it some more?"

"Fine."

"I was going to oil that chain, wasn't I?"

"You already did that. Can we go now?"

I'm jogging down the sidewalk behind Garrett, arm extended, hand clinging to the very edge of his seat. Just a couple days ago he still needed my assistance. Now, somehow, he's ready. I can feel it. "There, just like that," I say. "Ha-ha! Isn't this fun?"

"Yeah!" Garrett says, his hands gripping the handlebars, legs pushing and pulling, turning the pedals as he negotiates the sidewalk.

A teenager in a car races by out in the street, radio blaring and providing me a brief glimpse of the future. I want to hold on to the seat and never let go, but any moment now I'll have to release it, and there's nothing I can do about it.

It occurs to me that this happens only once in a lifetime. Once you learn to ride, you always remember.

"You're doing great," I say. "Just keep pedaling."

"You still holding on?" Garrett says.

"I'm holding on."

"Don't let go."

"Just keep pedaling," I say, my arm still extended, hand clamped precariously to the seat, to the seat...and then to nothing as I ease into a walk, straightening my back, feeling my heart pulsing in my chest, in my throat, wondering if I should sprint ahead to catch him, wondering if seven years is too early, too soon, and hoping, trusting, watching as Garrett turns the pedals, remembering my first real bike and the excitement, the uncertainty, of no training wheels, each pedal stroke a tiny victory as confidence slowly rolled into my mind, and now watching the same transformation in my son, watching instinct carry him along, his legs pushing and pulling him into life, into this great big world, and away from me.

He's now too far down the sidewalk, too far away for me to help him. He's on his own. And so am I. "Just keep pedaling," I say again, to myself, realizing as Garrett pedals farther and farther away that I'm losing something precious and fleeting, that in fact I've already lost it.

Migration

Sundown was less than an hour away and Joanne, the woman with the brown legs, had just returned with a jug of margaritas. Ed watched as she filled plastic cups for the others: the retired couple from Jacksonville, the college students who were laughing and snapping cell-phone pictures of themselves, the quiet Asian man with the autumnal smile: locals, mostly. Gradually, hands that had spent the day clutching binoculars and bird-watching guidebooks and tubes of sunscreen relinquished these objects and accepted the cocktails handed them until, at some point, the very tenor of the flock began to change. The skyward gazes and resolute faces from earlier in the day faded to convivial chatter, laughter, and a collective sense of resignation that the bird for which they'd all converged here on this tiny coastal park had already flown.

With the passing of each and every uneventful hour that afternoon, Ed had felt his sense of hope receding. Now it was nearly gone and in its place dismay and regret were beginning to set in, heavy and obtrusive, like the pounding hammers in the distance, the mass of condominiums spreading just beyond the park's northern boundary.

Then the bittersweet scent of the margaritas reached him and his breathing quickened. Ed adjusted the straps on his daypack, shifting the weight on his shoulders, as the salty-sweet scent seemed to hover in the air around him, colorful and timeless, like a photo album, reminding him of a trip to Mexico with his wife, Maureen–their first as a couple–taken sixteen years earlier, on their honeymoon. He took a deep breath as the memories surged through his mind, rattling his heart, and finally swirling into his stomach where they seemed to pool and harden. He saw himself holding hands with Maureen and pointing out tropical fish as they snorkeled over a reef; he felt the frenetic surprise of finding that secluded waterfall in the jungle; he tasted again the margaritas they'd sipped each evening as they watched the sun slip away and disappear. It was hard to believe this was sixteen years ago, and when Ed thought about it now it seemed to him those first years of marriage, before the mortgage, before the realization that they would never have children, and long before Maureen's cancer, were the happiest of his life. They'd made the most of this time without knowing they had to, without knowing she wouldn't live to see fifty.

Scanning the trees around him, his mind's eye caught the flitting image of he and Maureen here in this same park one afternoon, many years ago, counting the migrating warblers. The park was larger then, and Maureen, who'd grown up in nearby Delray Beach and spent countless hours here as a child, said it used to attract many more birds. What remained amounted to little more than a few precious acres of healthy habitat, and while this was a far cry from what it once was, in Ed's estimation the park's remaining stands of live oaks and gumbo limbos, and the quiet shade they afforded, offered a comfortable and welcome resting place nevertheless.

When Joanne offered Ed a margarita, he smiled and said no thanks, then lifted the field glasses to his eyes and peered into the canopy of the giant, gumbo limbo tree, whose red, flaky bark was peeling and falling away like time itself. Ed scanned the branches from left to right, right to left, higher and higher, and higher still, until he covered the entire tree and was staring now at the pink sky above as he listened for the rapid-fire *pit-pit-pit-pit* of the Cuban pewee, the source of his intrigue. Satisfied the tree was empty, he lowered the binoculars, checked his watch and, straining to hear the call that could still salvage this trip, mentally calculated the time it would take him to make it to the airport, return his rental car, clear TSA screening, and board the airliner that would carry him back to Illinois in time for work tomorrow morning.

"Come on, Eddie!" Joanne said as she refilled her cup. "Our little traveler's probably home by now. They just pass through," she said. "They don't stay long."

She was about Ed's age, late forties, tall and slender, with skin as brown as a cigar, which fascinated him. All day, she'd seemed to forego sunscreen, and yet she wasn't burned. Ed told himself it was just genetics. He told himself some people were just lucky, for three times that day he'd been forced to slather a coconut-smelling concoction with a sun-protection factor of fifty on his arms, neck, and face to protect his skin from the intense, subtropical sun. So had most of the others. Now he felt greasy and he was self-conscious about standing too close to this woman, who seemed so polished and poised, despite the long, hot day they'd spent here in the trees. Casually elegant was how he would have described her. Joanne seemed refined without trying to be, and she had those high cheekbones, and a way of rolling her vowels, stretching them, smoothing off their hard edges so that the words they formed seemed like gifts, polished and new, and unique, made just for Ed.

Yet, no matter how many verbal gifts she offered, Ed's eyes returned again and again to her smooth, brown skin, which he considered her most distinguishing feature. Increasingly, he longed for a hot shower.

As his eyes ascended into the sprawling gumbo limbo, it occurred to him that no one had called him Eddie since high school, although there'd been times over the years, in certain moments of passion or burning disagreement, when Maureen had shouted *Edward!* To everyone else, however, including his coworkers in the service department at the Toyota dealership back home, he was just Ed. Ordinary, everyday Ed, who'd taken a vacation day to fly down to Florida that morning after his favorite birding website posted a report of a Cuban pewee sighting in a tiny park of coastal scrub, live oaks, and gumbo limbos just north of Fort Lauderdale. *A rare opportunity to see this exotic species,* the report said. *Last confirmed sighting in the US was in 1995!*

Ed wanted to savor this day, but considering his lack of success thus far, he felt he was squandering it. Given the constraints of his impromptu trip, there was so much pressure. Any other time he might have accepted a margarita and resigned himself to a pleasant evening on the coast. But not now. Not in this situation. According to the report, there'd been a Cuban pewee in this park, among these trees, just the day before. And despite the setting sun and his impending flight, Ed was determined to see one.

"I've still got a half hour before I have to clear out," he said as he gripped the binoculars, twisting the focusing ring. "I might get lucky yet."

Joanne nodded and then took a long drink as the others grouped together across the clearing, talking and sipping their margaritas. A moment later she stepped closer to Ed. "I admire your determination," she said, her voice lower now. Then she placed her hand, very delicately, on his upper arm. "You seem stressed, though," she said. "You sure you won't have a drink?"

Looking through the binoculars, he said, "I'd better not. I still have to drive to the airport."

As he scanned the tree, he heard the ice cubes rattling in her cup. Then she said, "These birds. They're never here for very long," she said. "I used to keep records of what I saw, like I was trying to keep score or something. But I've since learned it's best to come out here without any expectations and just enjoy. That's the real gift in all this, I think."

"I wish I had more time," Ed said. "Another day or so." Now he lowered the binoculars and glanced at Joanne, whose face glowed in the warm evening light. Then, looking into the trees, he said, "I'd really like to see this bird before I go back."

Joanne directed her gaze across the clearing, toward the others, and shook her cup. "Keep your eyes open," she said. "You might get lucky after all."

Ed felt the blood rush to his face. Unsure how to respond, he lifted the binoculars to his eyes and held them there for what seemed a long time before pulling them away. When he did, Joanne had the cup turned up. Most arresting, however, was the angle of her head, tilted back, her delicate throat exposed, eyes closed as if asleep. Again, Ed looked into the tree, taking a deep breath and holding, holding, then exhaling slowly in an effort to steady the binoculars.

"I guess it's about time to head to the beach," Joanne said a moment later. "We always start here on the trail, and by sunset we're down by the water. You should have a drink and join us. I think our Cuban friend's split."

"If I had more time, I'd love to," Ed said, reveling in the sound of her voice, her apparent warmth and understanding, and the thought that these smooth, polished words had been made just for him. And for the first time, he thought of staying. Just one more day.

"I understand," she said. "It's been very nice to meet you." She extended her arms and Ed turned to her and they hugged. There was a certain confidence, but also a cool indifference, in these arms, and her scent lingered in Ed's nose even after they let go. He told himself he needed a shower. "We'll be down on the beach if you change your mind," she said.

Ed watched her walk across the clearing to the others.

Joanne was a local. If she missed her bird, she could come back tomorrow, or next week, and find another. But tomorrow morning Ed would be draining the incinerated oil from a Camry and wondering if his failure was the result of a false sighting, poor timing, or something else. Glancing over the treetops, he could see the peaks of the new condominium development taking shape, growing, spreading like the skin cancer that had taken Maureen, his wife and best friend, the green-eyed girl he'd wooed, who'd introduced him to birding and had always wanted to see a Cuban pewee herself.

Here was Ed's opportunity to live one of Maureen's dreams for her, and yet, despite a solid report and nearly eight hours on location, he'd come up empty. He told himself he was failing her.

He peered again through the treetops at the development in the near distance. He wondered how much longer this tiny stand of vegetation might resist the builders' dozers. How much longer until even this was razed to make way for more condominiums? And then where would the migrating birds go?

On the opposite side of the woodlot, traffic sliced along the highway, producing a soft hissing noise as Ed scanned the branches, still listening for the bird's telltale *pit-pit-pit-pit*. The voices of the others had grown softer, more distant, and when he next looked the group was halfway down the trail, headed toward the beach. Joanne had removed her flip-flops and walked barefoot through the sand, holding the shoes in one hand, the red cup in the other. Ed felt a knot in his throat. He wanted to call out to her or follow her down to the beach. But he stood fast, gripping the binoculars, his fingers twisting the focusing ring back and forth, over and over.

A moment later the group rounded a bend in the trail and disappeared, and Ed's mind throbbed with the pressure of his time constraints. Finally, he released the binoculars and turned as if to set off toward the beach. Instead, he loosened the straps on his daypack and felt the weight slide down his arms.

Alone in the fast-expiring daylight, Ed removed a small, gray box from his daypack and held it in his hands, trying to gather himself as apologies flitted about his mind. He told himself he'd failed. He told himself he'd done his best given the circumstances. Looking down the trail, the sounds of distant hammers still pounding in his ears, he told himself he had to do this before it was too late, before one of the others came stumbling back, before his boarding time called him away, before the developers excised this park from the coast, like a surgeon with a scalpel, as if it had never existed. Now he opened the box and stepped forward, watching as the trees and the earth absorbed his wife, insulating her in their cool shade and leaving him instantly and irrevocably alone as another piece of the gumbo limbo bark fell away to the ground where it landed with a *tick*.

John Gifford lives in Oklahoma City. He has worked as a furniture mover, feed-store manager, angling consultant, in television production, as a safety and risk manager, U.S. Marine, and as a corporate writer. He holds a master of fine arts degree from the University of Central Oklahoma, and a BA from the University of Oklahoma, where he received the Goldia Cooksey Memorial Award for creative writing. His work has appeared in *Southwest Review*, *Louisiana Literature*, *Cold Mountain Review*, *The Christian Science Monitor* and elsewhere.